Prologue

It probably never, ever would have happened in a million years without the huge blustery blizzard that brought the whole big city to a stop. The eighteen inches of snow gave five fifth-grade girls the chance to become best friends overnight. Their names are Megan, Keisha, Alison, Rosa and Heather. They are not very much alike—hardly at all. But after that night, they have a great discovery in common. It's something they keep to themselves because most adults would wonder if the girls had gone crazy! They might think the girls had let their imaginations run wild, and say: "Be real now, girls. You know an attic can't be magic."

But it is. It's magic enough to send Megan, Keisha, Alison, Rosa and Heather on the most wonderful one-of-a-kind adventures.

Contents

1

Stranded!

The whole room went dark. Some of the kids let out a scream, but not Megan Ryder. It's just a blackout, Megan thought to herself, and two seconds later Mr. Preston, the school superintendent, said the same thing.

"Children! Please listen." Mr. Preston raised his voice over the noise of the confusion. "The blizzard has knocked out the power to the hotel. Please sit back down."

Megan seemed to be the only one paying attention to Mr. Preston. She could hear people bumping into each other all over the place, trying to move around in the dark. No one was saying "excuse me" or "sorry."

Suddenly there was a whirring sound and a buzz and a click, and a couple of kids screamed again until two giant spotlights that looked like car headlights came on over the doors.

"That's the emergency generator kicking in," Kyle said, from the seat next to Megan's. Kyle Dresden was the other student council member from Downey Elementary, where Megan attended fifth grade. More than sixty kids, from many different nearby schools, had been invited downtown that morning to the old Parker hotel for a student get-together in the big conference room. It was Mr. Preston's idea. He was brand-new at his job and decided it would be a good idea to hear from fifth and sixth graders on how to make the school system better.

"Before lunch we will hear each person's suggestions," Mr. Preston had announced when they had all arrived that morning. "Then, after lunch, we will all go ice skating on the new rink near city hall."

Everyone seemed excited about the skating part of the day. Some of the kids even brought their own ice skates. Megan didn't have any. She had only been ice skating three times in her life. The first two times she had skated around the outer edge, hanging on to the wall. The third time she had managed to take baby steps into the center of the rink. Megan had felt embarrassed because some very little kids were gliding by her and doing spins. She couldn't even stand on skates without her ankles flopping out to the sides. But she still looked forward to the afternoon because there would be no math problems to solve. If Megan were at school today she would have to work on multiplying fractions, which she was horrible at. Instead, she would be sailing around the rink or—more likely—taking baby steps with flip-floppy ankles.

It seemed like the first part of the day went on and on, way too long. There was a lot of talk about things like "too much homework" and "not enough school spirit" and parent-teacher nights and smelly lockers because of tuna fish sandwiches, and scratchy paper towels in the bathrooms.

Megan was nervous standing in front of the group, so she shared her ideas quickly.

"Number one," Megan said, wondering if the other kids could see her knees shaking behind her white tights. "Math class would be more interesting if it was shown as a movie, like history is sometimes."

Megan tucked her long hair behind her ears and then took it back out. She was pretty sure her ears were bright red. "Number two," she continued. "Field trips are always something about science, which gets boring. At least two trips every year should involve horses, or maybe going to a mall to hang out."

All the girls in the room cheered and clapped for that suggestion. Mr. Preston and the other adults just scrunched their eyebrows and wrote it down on their yellow pads of paper.

Next it was Kyle's turn to stand in the front. The first thing he said was, "Girls are weird." All the girls booed and hissed at that.

Mr. Preston said very sternly, "People!" and everyone got real quiet.

Kyle was a sixth grader who acted like he should get to skip grade school, junior high and high school and just go straight to college. That's how cool Kyle thought he was. Some other kids thought he was cool, too, because he always had new clothes from expensive stores. Megan thought he was pretty much of a pain because he usually teased her badly, but her mom said it was a sure sign that he liked her.

That just doesn't make sense, Megan thought, wondering if her mother had any idea what it was like to be ten.

Kyle gave his first idea. "Skate-board ramps should be added to the playground and if a kickball goes on top of any school building during a game that should count as an automatic homerun."

Kyle did a high five with one of the boys sitting in the front row.

"Is that it?" Mr. Preston asked, after all the boys were done cheering.

"One more thing," Kyle added, tugging on the belt of his long baggy pants, "cool music should be played during the morning announcements to make them more interesting."

Just as all the boys and some of the girls were clapping for Kyle's music suggestion a man who worked at the hotel interrupted the meeting. He told Mr. Preston to come to the lobby with him to look out of the window, since there were no windows at all in the big conference room.

That's when they discovered there was a giant blizzard outside. All the news programs were saying that the forecast of three inches of snow was turning into the worst blizzard in fifteen years. Everyone should go home now—or risk getting trapped.

"Many parents have already arrived to take you home," Mr. Preston said. "Please put on your coats and check out with me."

"What about the skating?" a girl with long blonde hair asked, holding up her skates with the laces tied together.

"I'm afraid it's cancelled," Mr. Preston replied. "I'm sure the rink has been shut down for the day."

Some of the kids groaned, but most just grabbed their backpacks and left quickly, while nervous parents said things like: "Hurry. Hurry. We don't want to get stuck." Many of the adults called out "good luck" to each other as they left.

When Mr. Preston counted how many children remained there were six boys and five girls, including Megan.

Megan knew her mother wouldn't be picking her up because she was at a courthouse two hours away, working on a case. Megan's mother was a lawyer, and was busy with work all day and sometimes all evening until midnight. Megan's mom had arranged for her to ride home from the city with Kyle's mother.

"My mom is going to pick us up on her way home from the airport," Kyle told Mr. Preston. "She's in Phoenix on a business trip."

"I've been told the airport is closed now, too," Mr. Preston said. "Looks like your mom is stuck in sunny Arizona for another day."

Kyle's dad was at home taking care of Kyle's baby brother and Megan's dad was in Brazil covering a news story about the rainforest. Her parents were divorced and she only got to see her dad when he was in the country. He always made sure he spent some time with her before every foreign assignment.

"I think we're officially stranded," Megan told Kyle.

"No, duh! Troll girl," Kyle answered.

Kyle called Megan "troll girl" because she was much shorter than Kyle and had long, straight strawberry-blonde hair. One time Kyle sneaked up behind her on the front steps of the school and held her ponytail up straight above her head. "See," he said, "you look just like a troll."

Megan called him "Kyle Crocodile" sometimes because, she told him, "you have a really big mouth."

Mr. Preston said to the remaining children, "Please sit at the table and eat your lunch while the adults figure out what to do."

Even though it was way past their usual lunchtime, nobody was really hungry, But what else could they do? Megan sat next to Kyle and opened her lunch bag.

"Are you going to start crying?" Kyle asked Megan, as he ran the palm of his hand over the top of his spiky gelled hair. "Just let me know if you're going to start sobbing like a baby troll, so I can sit somewhere else."

Megan wanted to say something quick like "you wish" or "only if I'm stuck with you, Kyle Crocodile," but the truth was, she really did feel like crying. Instead, she unwrapped her peanut butter sandwich and took a bite. She wasn't sure she could swallow over the big lump in her throat.

Megan decided to ignore Kyle because she had enough to think about. She had to figure out a way to get home. She looked down at her leather boots and wondered if she could walk through deep snowdrifts for more than eleven miles. She didn't even have a hat or a scarf. She was glad she had at least dressed in her favorite thick yellow sweater with the fluffy yarn cuffs and collar.

Then she remembered her mom in the car that morning asking, "Honey, don't you want your hat? It might snow."

Megan had put her hand up flat in the air to stop any further discussion. "No one in fifth grade wears a hat, mother."

She had started calling her mom "mother" on Thanksgiving Day. She didn't really know why, but it was probably because she finally got to eat at the big table. She was so happy she didn't have to sit at the little wooden table in tiny red plastic chairs with her messy pre-school cousins, who were just learning how to use silverware. Megan thought "mommy" sounded

too babyish for the adult table, especially since she got to sit next to Aunt Maggie, who had great manners and even knew which was the salad fork and which fork was for the mashed potatoes.

And then, just as Megan was thinking about Aunt Maggie and how she always tucked her napkin into the waistband of her skirt, the door to the conference room opened with a bang. Everyone stopped in the middle of their chewing and stared at the doorway.

Mrs. Outlandish to the Rescue!

*C*an I help you?" Mr. Preston asked, squinting at a stranger standing in the glare of the two emergency spotlights.

"Miss Megan Ryder, please. I've come to collect her." The stranger's voice boomed across the room in a most dramatic way.

Some of the kids blinked three or four times, as if they thought they were dreaming. Before their very eyes stood Mrs. Outlandish, the most popular character in "Action Expedition." And "Action Expedition," as any kid would tell you, was the best show on television.

Megan rolled up her lunch bag, grabbed her backpack and headed for the door. Everyone in the room jumped up and followed. Megan was the only one not yelling: "Mrs. Outlandish! Mrs. Outlandish!"

Even Mr. Preston stood with his mouth hanging open and finally said, "I can't believe…it's really Maggie Carmody."

Kyle caught up with Megan: "You know Mrs. Outlandish? A troll girl like you!"

"Yes," Megan answered. "But, she's not…"

She didn't even get to finish before Kyle ran off to get an autograph.

Megan didn't run. For Megan, the person at the door wasn't Mrs. Outlandish, she was just her aunt.

Aunt Maggie was her mom's oldest sister. She was fourteen years older and usually called Megan's mom "Baby" instead of Julia, which was her name.

Not only was Aunt Maggie the oldest in the family, she was also the tallest: six feet one inch and a half to be exact. Megan's mom always said, "Maggie got the tall skeleton and a ton of talent to fill it up." Even her feet were big, size eleven and a half, to be exact. And not only was Aunt Maggie the oldest and the tallest in the family, she was also the most famous. It was hard to find anyone who hadn't heard of Maggie Carmody. She had starred in a long list of plays and movies in the thirty years she had been an actress. One year ago Aunt Maggie was offered what Megan thought was the best part of her whole career: the daring and crazy explorer Mrs. Outlandish in "Action Expedition."

"One at a time, please," Aunt Maggie was telling the children who circled around her, holding pieces of notebook paper up to her face. Without taking off her leopard-print gloves, Aunt Maggie signed autographs.

Megan squeezed her way up to her aunt's side and tugged on her bright purple scarf with the silky tassels. "Here I am, Aunt Maggie. Boy, am I glad to see you. Are you taking me home?"

Aunt Maggie stared right at Megan with her leaf-green eyes and said, "Absolutely not!"

Now Megan could really feel the lump in her throat getting bigger. Why was Aunt Maggie there if she wasn't going to take her home? She could feel her eyes, which were the same green color as Aunt Maggie's, getting watery.

Mr. Preston was the last one waiting for an autograph. He looked embarrassed and shy instead of like an important school superintendent.

"I…you…I…," Mr. Preston stumbled.

"Yes? " Aunt Maggie responded, pushing her curly reddish hair back under her wide-rimmed black hat.

"You're my biggest fan!" Mr. Preston blurted.

He looked even more flustered when all the children laughed.

Aunt Maggie laughed, too. "Perhaps I am your biggest fan."

"Oh, no!" Mr. Preston cried. His forehead got a little sweaty. "I meant I'm *your* biggest fan."

He shook his head side to side at his own goof-up. Aunt Maggie put her arm around his shoulder and said, "There, there, it's okay. I understand. "

Mr. Preston looked down at his black shiny shoes and said, "You're very, very nice, Maggie Carmody."

Then Aunt Maggie said: "What's to be done here? Megan's mother called to see if I could rescue Megan, which I'm most delighted to do."

"You are?" Megan asked.

"Of course," Aunt Maggie said, bending down quite a bit to kiss Megan on the cheek. "I live just five blocks from here, so we'll have a sleepover at my place. Sounds like fun, don't you think?"

"I'd like that a lot," Megan answered.

"It looks like Megan isn't the only one stranded here in the city." Aunt Maggie scanned the crowd.

Mr. Preston spoke up. "The other parents have been calling. Many of them can't get here because of the snow. My wife and I live downtown, so she told me to bring them all home with me tonight."

"Absolutely not!" Aunt Maggie said again. "The

girls will come with me and the boys will go with you."

"But…I…you…" Mr. Preston was stumbling over his words again.

"That is that! It's a wrap." Aunt Maggie clapped her hands as if a movie scene had ended.

Kyle stepped forward. "I'd like to go with Mrs. Outlandish."

Mr. Preston said: "No, Kyle. You'll stay with the boys tonight."

Kyle did not like that answer. He looked at Megan and scowled.

Megan leaned over and whispered: "Are you going to start crying?"

"Hey," Kyle said, but then he grinned. "I guess I was asking for that."

Megan felt a little bit sorry for Kyle so she unrolled her lunch bag and took out her chocolate chip cookie. "Here," she said handing it to him, " a crocodile cookie."

Kyle took the cookie and put the whole thing in his mouth at once. Then, with his mouth completely full, he said, "girls are still weird." But it came out, along with bits of chocolate chip cookie, as, "gris or stow wired."

Aunt Maggie frowned. "Words and food should never come out of a mouth at the same time."

Kyle said, "I'm sawwy. Reewy, reewy sawwy." More cookie sprayed out as he talked.

All the boys were laughing. The girls were saying things like "sick" and "yuck."

Aunt Maggie, pretending her mouth was full, replied, "Apowagy accepted."

Mr. Preston laughed the hardest at that one.

After Aunt Maggie had talked to each of the girl's parents on the phone, saying every time: "It's no bother" and "Here's my phone number" and "I'd be happy to send you an autographed photo," they were finally ready to go.

"Before we head out into the vast tundra," Aunt Maggie said, "tell me your names while you put on your coats."

The first girl who spoke was a little taller than Megan, with dark-brown eyes, long black hair and skin the color of creamy hot chocolate. Her purple striped shirt and cargo pants gave her an adventurous look.

"I'm Keisha Vance and I live in Overland and I'm ten and I'm the oldest of the three kids in my family."

"Well," Aunt Maggie said, "that's a very long name! Nice to meet you Keisha Vance and I live in Overland and I'm ten…"

All the girls started to giggle and for the first time

they all took a real true look at each other. Megan noticed right away that the blonde girl who had brought her own ice skates was with them. She was wearing a denim jacket that looked great with her blue eyes. "What's your name?" Megan asked her.

"Alison McCann."

Next to her was a girl with very pretty brown eyes and long dark hair that spread across the ruffles of her lime green shirt.

"Hi, everybody. I'm Rosa Garcia. Thanks for inviting me over, Mrs. Outlan...I mean...Mrs....um."

Aunt Maggie shook Rosa's hand. "All of you may call me Aunt Maggie. That will keep it simple. Now, we just need to know your name, young lady."

A girl who seemed to be very shy stood a little off to the side. Megan remembered she had acted very nervous when she had to share suggestions.

The girls and Aunt Maggie all turned to look at her. Her mouth was moving, but no sound was coming out.

"Has a cat got your tongue, or are you eating a giant cookie, too?" asked Aunt Maggie.

The girl looked like she could start to cry.

Aunt Maggie knelt down and put her hands on the girl's shoulders. "Let's see. Yes, I do believe a very clever tabby cat is trying to sneak away with your tongue. Shoo, kitty. Go catch mice!"

The other girls all laughed.

Aunt Maggie gathered the girl's long brown hair in her hands and moved it away from her face.

"What a lovely pink sweater. And matching boots! An excellent touch!"

"My name's Heather. Heather Hardin," the girl said, finally starting to smile.

Aunt Maggie shook Heather's hand and said, "Very nice to make your acquaintance." Then she stood up. "All right, Heather Hardin, please pair up with Rosa Garcia. Alison McCann, please buddy up with Keisha Vance, and Megan Ryder, you shall be my companion on this trek. We're off, ingenues."

Rosa looked around at the other girls. "An-ja-what? Is that a compliment or an insult?"

Keisha, Alison and Heather all shrugged.

Megan was not puzzled, because she had grown up with Aunt Maggie and knew some of the words that theatre people used.

"An ingenue is another word for young lady, like a young actress," she explained.

"Not just young, but innocent." Aunt Maggie added. "All right, now," she clapped her hands. "If we know what's for our own good we better get going before it's too late. If the snow gets any deeper, it will be over your heads! Now follow me."

Aunt Maggie left the conference room and started across the big lobby. As she walked, she held her head up high and her shoulders were straight, but one hip went a little further to the side. This made her stride have a little bump right in the middle of it.

Keisha, following, asked, "Do you have a blister from your boots?"

"Absolutely not," said Aunt Maggie. "You're probably asking that because of the way I walk."

Megan wondered if her aunt was embarrassed by the question. If she was, it didn't show on her face. But then, Aunt Maggie was a great actress.

"I had an accident when I was a young woman," Aunt Maggie said, "and now my right leg is a bit shorter than my left leg. That's why I walk with an unusual gait."

"What happened?" Keisha asked.

"Perhaps you'll find out someday," said Aunt Maggie.

"Okay. Whatever," Keisha said.

Megan noticed that the answer didn't bother Keisha, and silently admired her boldness in asking what she wanted to know. Aunt Maggie was used to being asked many questions because she was famous, but Megan had never heard her answer this one.

Aunt Maggie pushed open the door and they stepped into a world where everything looked like a giant wedding cake. It was snowing in every direction and wind gusts blew the snow right into their faces.

Megan gripped Aunt Maggie's hand, and tried to put her nose and mouth into the top of her own coat. The snow on the sidewalk was so deep it came over the tops of her boots. The girls and Aunt Maggie plodded through drift after drift.

They passed a flower truck stuck in a bank of snow at the side of the street. It was very strange to see the brightly colored flowers when everything else around them was white. The parking meters looked like big cotton swabs and the cars next to the curbs looked like sleeping polar bears.

"Only one more block!" Aunt Maggie shouted into the wind towards the girls. Then she stopped.

"Hold on!" she ordered, looking very concerned. "Where's Rosa?"

Megan, Alison and Keisha all turned around to look at Heather who was holding Rosa's bright-red, but empty, mitten.

Heather's mouth moved, but no sound came out. Keisha said, "Uh-oh. This isn't good."

Alison said, "Exactly."

Megan said, "Where could she have gone?"

Aunt Maggie dropped Megan's hand and went over to Heather, who looked more afraid than ever. She leaned her ear down to Heather's mouth.

"Tell me where Rosa has gone. Don't be afraid." Then she listened for a moment and nodded.

"All right, ingenues," she said. "It seems that Rosa left us a ways back."

Heather spoke out loud. "I'm so sorry. She let go of my hand and I called to her, but she didn't stay with me. I was scared I would get left behind, too. I thought she would catch up with us, but she didn't."

Aunt Maggie looked very, very worried for a minute, and then said, "We will retrace our steps until we find her."

Alison asked, "All of us?"

"If we were in a play, could the play go on without one of the actors?" Aunt Maggie asked in return.

The girls all shook their heads.

"Then we will all go back, until we can all go on together. Are we in agreement?"

All the girls nodded.

Megan looked at Aunt Maggie's face. She could tell that Aunt Maggie was extremely worried about

Rosa, but she was putting on a brave face.

The girls all held hands again and started trudging back through the snow. As they walked, they called out Rosa's name. Aunt Maggie made her name much longer by rolling on the "R," and really boomed it out. "R-R-R-Rosaaaa!"

A short, older man came towards them. He had an inch of snow on his cap and his glasses needed windshield wipers.

"Excuse me, sir," Megan stepped in his path. "Have you seen a girl about my size with long brown hair?"

The man was rather grumpy. "I can't see a thing, young lady. My glasses are fogged over and caked with snow." Then he stopped, took off his glasses and looked at the group. "Wait a minute. Are you Maggie Carmody, the famous Maggie Carmody? You're a very good actress."

Aunt Maggie looked directly at him and said, "Today I am Aunt Maggie, thank you. But not a very good aunt, obviously. If you'll excuse me, I have a pressing matter to attend to."

They continued on, beginning to shiver now in the snow. Finally they could see the flower truck ahead of them. Alison suddenly shouted out, "Look, up ahead. It looks like Rosa's other mitten on top of that snow bank." She handed her ice skates to Megan and ran ahead, jumping over snowdrifts and zigzagging between parking meters. Then she climbed a snow bank and disappeared down the other side.

Keisha looked up at Aunt Maggie, shook her head slowly and said, "There goes another one. It looks like we're down to four of us."

Aunt Maggie's voice boomed even louder: "Allll-iissssssoonnnn! R-R-R-Rossssaaaa!"

"Alison is fast," Heather remarked. "Maybe if she was Rosa's partner, Rosa would have never got lost."

Megan held on to Heather's hand tightly. She felt very sorry for her. It could have happened to anyone, but she knew Heather felt terrible.

Alison's head popped back up over a bank of snow and she started waving both arms.

"I've found her!"

"Thank you," Aunt Maggie said, turning her face to the sky. Megan could tell her aunt was saying a short prayer.

When the group got next to the flower truck they could see all of Alison, but only Rosa's head. The rest of Rosa's body had disappeared under the truck.

"Are you hurt?" Aunt Maggie asked, climbing the snow bank and then getting on her knees in the snow.

"No. But I can't get out. It's too slippery." Rosa answered. Her teeth were chattering badly.

"Well, you do look buried, and there are lots of flowers over your head. But I don't think it's your time to go, do you?" Aunt Maggie didn't wait for an answer. "Help me now, ingenues," she directed.

All of the girls reached under the truck and grabbed a part of Rosa's coat. "On the count of three, give a giant pull. One…two…three."

With one long movement, Rosa was out from under the truck. The girls cheered, but Rosa started crying.

Aunt Maggie sat down on the snow, unbuttoned her coat and pulled Rosa inside it. Rosa buried her head in Aunt Maggie's shoulder and cried some more.

"All right, now," Aunt Maggie said, patting Rosa's back. "Everyone is safe."

Between sobs, Rosa told how she had let go of Heather's hand because she knew the flowers would freeze with the truck door open. She went to close it, slipped down the snow bank and under the truck.

Keisha said, "It's a good thing the truck was stuck in the snow, too. Or you'd be a pancake!"

Aunt Maggie gave Keisha a look that said no one needed to be reminded of that, and then told Rosa it was time to dry her tears because there was quite enough moisture around already.

Rosa smiled a little, and put her hands in the red mittens Heather offered.

Aunt Maggie stood up, buttoned her coat and held out her hands to Rosa and Megan.

"Happy ending," she said. "Now let's get out of this storm."

Nobody let go of anybody's hand, and nobody did any more talking until they stood together in front of a reddish-brown brick building with eight big windows.

3

Mrs. Outlandish at Home

ou live in a mansion!" Keisha said, as they climbed the front steps.

"This is much bigger than my house," Rosa remarked, "and we have seven in my family, almost eight. My mama is having a baby in three more months."

"I wish my mom was having a baby," Megan said. "I'd love a brother or sister."

Aunt Maggie let a funny snort out through her nose and said, "Anything is possible. After all, my little sister came along when I was fourteen years old."

Megan grinned up at Aunt Maggie because she was talking about Megan's mom. Megan was glad her mom had such a great big sister.

Aunt Maggie pushed open the front door and all the girls came into the entryway, stomping the snow off their boots on the doormat. Megan had been to Aunt Maggie's house once when she was four or five years old. She didn't remember it being so big.

"This building is what you call a three flat," Aunt Maggie announced. "That means that there are three apartments, one on each floor. On this bottom floor is Mrs. Silver. She lives by herself, except for her pet."

Aunt Maggie knocked on the first-floor door. A minute later an older lady in a homemade wrap-around shawl answered the door. She was carrying a small gray cat in her arms. Her face broke into a re-lieved smile when she saw Aunt Maggie.

"Oh, Maggie," Mrs. Silver said, "I'm so happy you're back home safe."

Aunt Maggie said, "Thank you. And, as you can see, I am with quite a lot of company, all stranded in the blizzard. One of them is my niece, but they're all so covered with snow I'm not sure which one."

Megan stepped forward, holding up her hand. "That would be me."

Mrs. Silver remarked, "Yes, yes. I can see the re-semblance. You both have those lively green eyes, and that strawberry hair. Some people say I resemble my cat, HiHo." she said, holding up the sleepy cat. "I guess I do. We're both old and gray."

The girls all laughed at that.

"Your cat is named HiHo?" Heather asked.

"Yes," said Mrs Silver, "When I come home, I call out to him, "HiHo Silver.""

"And away!" Aunt Maggie finished, waving her hat up in the air above her head like a cowboy and laughing. Aunt Maggie explained to the girls. "You see, Mrs. Silver always calls herself a lone ranger."

"You're not alone," Keisha said. "You've got HiHo."

"And wonderful friends," Mrs. Silver said, winking at Aunt Maggie.

Heather reached up to pet HiHo's head.

"I just love cats. My mom said maybe I can get one when I turn twelve," Heather said.

"Until then you can visit HiHo Silver anytime. He loves to be cuddled," Mrs. Silver said.

"I have a cat. My oldest brother, Carlos, found her," Rosa said, finally done shivering. "Her name is Bonita. That's the Spanish word for pretty."

"Very clever," Mrs. Silver said smiling.

"My cat is named Ginger. She sleeps in a basket next to my bed. I also really like horses. No—I love horses. But I don't have one," Megan added.

"Oh," said Mrs. Silver. "I do, too. But, I don't have one, either. It's hard to keep one in an apartment.

They don't fit in a basket like a cat does."

Megan giggled along with the other girls, thinking how funny a horse in a basket would look.

"If you need anything, Mrs. Silver, please call," Aunt Maggie said.

"Thank you, dear. I'm fine. I know you'll have a very interesting evening, girls. It seems like I was a girl just a short while ago and I remember how much fun it can be," Mrs. Silver answered, with a sparkle in her eye.

The girls waved goodbye and followed Aunt Maggie up the stairs to the second floor.

"This is where the Delgados live. There's Raymond and Mellie and their children, who are in high school, Katia and Luis."

"I wonder if they're Hispanic, like me," Rosa asked.

"I believe Raymond came here from Mexico when he was about your age," Aunt Maggie answered. "They are a very nice family and we've become good friends. And I'd like to keep it that way. So we should remember that we will be walking on their ceiling."

"We will?" Alison asked. "Upside down? I'm pretty athletic, but I don't think I could do that."

"Absolutely not," Aunt Maggie said. "We will be in my apartment which is above theirs. That means my floor is on top of their ceiling. Understand?"

"Exactly," Alison replied.

When they reached the third floor, Aunt Maggie pulled her key ring from her coat pocket. It was filled with keys, but one old-fashioned-looking golden one caught Megan's eye.

"What's that key for, Aunt Maggie?" Megan asked, as the other girls leaned in to have a look.

"Ah. That's a very special key to one of my very favorite places." Aunt Maggie told her. "I'll show you all later this evening. But first you must meet Monty."

"Is Monty your husband?" Heather asked.

Megan covered her mouth so that Heather wouldn't see her giggle. She knew who Monty was, because he went nearly everywhere with Aunt Maggie.

"No, he's not my husband. We would certainly make an odd-looking couple," Aunt Maggie said.

She unlocked the door and sitting right at the doorway was the cutest little dog, an all-white West Highland Terrier.

Monty barked a hello and wagged his tail. Then he took to sniffing each of the girl's boots.

"It's a good thing you weren't with me today, my little Monty," Aunt Maggie said. "We almost lost a whole girl in the blizzard. Since you are small and white I may have misplaced you for good."

With that, Aunt Maggie bent down and scooped up Monty, who licked hellos all over her face.

Then she said, "Kick off your boots, ingenues, put them on this newspaper and hang your coats on this rack. I'll get you towels to dry your hair. It's unfortunate that fifth graders don't wear hats."

The girls looked at each other and smirked. How did she know?

"Look around if you'd like," Aunt Maggie said, walking away down the hall, with that slight bump in her step.

The apartment was both old and new. The floors were made of dark stained wood and there were throw rugs everywhere, some with bright colors and long threads, and some that were flat with tiny flowers. There was a very hip-looking brown leather couch next to a green-and-yellow Tiffany lamp, which sat on an old-fashioned washstand table with a big bowl and water pitcher on the lower shelf. Next to the couch was a rocking chair with hand-painted leaves on the arms and the back.

A music stand stood in one corner, next to a large instrument case that leaned against the wall. At the end of the room was one of the huge windows the girls had noticed from the front of the building. Near

it was a long bench that looked like an old church pew, with velvet and silk pillows all over it. What was most amazing was the number of books in the room. There were two huge bookshelves built right into the wall, reaching all the way to the ceiling.

"Wow," Alison remarked. "It would take me forever to read all these books."

Megan thought about how she would love to read forever, never do another math problem, just read interesting books.

Rosa touched a row of books as far up as she could reach. "My Nana told me that a person with a lot of books is rich in wisdom."

Keisha said, "Well, we know Aunt Maggie's rich. She must be. She's famous."

Heather just stood in the middle of the room.

"Are you all right?" Megan said. "You look like you can't talk again."

"Oh, sorry," said Heather. "I'm just surprised. I thought her house would be full of gold and fancy paintings and chandeliers and marble statues."

"Me, too," Keisha added. "And I thought she would have a butler and someone to paint her fingernails."

Just then Aunt Maggie came around the corner with towels. "I probably should have someone do my fingernails," she said. "They never come out right. I always want to do something else before the polish dries and then they get all splotched. So I don't bother."

Megan called the other girls into the hallway again. "Look at all my aunt's awards. Here's her Golden Choice award for a movie." Megan felt happy to have an aunt with such an exciting life.

The girls rushed to a long table in the hallway that held at least ten awards. Heather ran her fingers along the bottom of a tall shiny one.

"This one says Best Actress, Maggie Carmody."

On the wall over the table were many framed pictures of Aunt Maggie on stage, in movie scenes and at opening-night parties. Keisha pointed at one. "Look! Here's a picture of you as Mrs. Outlandish!"

Alison twisted a towel around her long blonde hair to dry it. "I've won two soccer trophies. One for my third-grade team and one last year. They're my favorite things. I bet you look at these everyday," she said, looking up into Aunt Maggie's face.

Aunt Maggie was holding a simple curved piece of clear glass with words engraved in it. "This is the only one that really matters to me."

Keisha crinkled up her nose. "That plain old piece of glass?"

"Why don't you read this out loud?" Aunt Maggie asked Keisha, handing her the award.

Keisha read slowly and carefully. "It says: To Maggie Carmody, for her great humanitarian efforts towards funding the Hope Harbor Shelter for Women and Children."

"What's a humanitarian? Is that like a vegetarian?" Heather asked.

"And what's Hope Harbor? Is that a TV show?" Rosa wanted to know.

"A humanitarian is a person of good will, one who is generous," Aunt Maggie answered. "And Hope Harbor is a place where women and children who don't have a home can go to get some help."

Megan joined in. "Every year Aunt Maggie has a big performance that raises money for Hope Harbor. I always go. It's a lot of funny skits and singing and dancing."

"Oh, I love watching dancing," said Heather. "I might get to take lessons this year. That is, if we get to stay in the house we live in now. I really like my new neighborhood."

"Should Heather go to Hope Harbor if she doesn't get to stay in her house?" Rosa asked Aunt Maggie.

"Heather means she's moving, I think. Is that

right?" Aunt Maggie turned to Heather.

"My father works for the airlines. We move all the time," Heather answered, nodding her head. "I never get to keep the friends I make."

"I get it," Keisha said, making a point by putting her finger up in the air. "That's why you're shy and I'm not. We've always lived in the same house. Everybody knows me. Sometimes that's not a good thing. The neighbors always tell my Mom and Dad what I'm up to. Once, I climbed out my bedroom window when I was grounded for using bad language and my dad was at the end of the driveway, just waiting for me to come around the corner. He was so mad, I thought he was going to use some bad language himself. But he didn't!"

Aunt Maggie said, "Well, please don't jump out of a window tonight. We are three floors up."

"Don't worry. I won't," Keisha replied.

Megan said, "The women Aunt Maggie helps don't have anywhere to live. They don't have money or any family to take care of them."

Rosa looked very sad. She bent down to rub Monty's furry belly as he flopped over onto his back. "Even dogs and cats get to live in houses. I think everyone should have a home."

"I agree," said Aunt Maggie. "That's why it makes

me feel good, much better than any award, to help other women."

"I help my mama and my Nana with housework and sometimes cooking," Rosa said.

"And I have to help my little brothers," Alison said. "They're seven and they're twins. They really make me crazy, sometimes."

"I know how that goes," Keisha said. "I have a little brother and a little sister. They ask me questions all the time."

"Helping your family is an excellent way to start becoming a humanitarian," Aunt Maggie said. "Now, maybe I should show some generosity and get you girls something to eat. I bet you would all love some delicious pizza."

"That sounds good," said Heather. "With lots and lots of cheese."

"Exactly!" said Alison. "How about sausage?"

"And pepperoni!" Keisha added.

"Yeah!" The other girls cheered.

"Well, that's very unfortunate," said Aunt Maggie, turning and heading to the kitchen. "I don't have pizza. But I did make a whole kettle of vegetable soup this morning."

"Vegetable?" Rosa asked.

"Soup?" said Heather.

"Yes, vegetable soup!" said Aunt Maggie, without looking back. "Vegetables are those green, orange and yellow pieces of food that many children pretend they don't like."

"Is your aunt a vegetarian humanitarian?" Keisha asked Megan as they followed Aunt Maggie.

"I saw her eat turkey a couple of times," Megan whispered. "At Thanksgiving. Come on, I'll ask her if she has some bologna and potato chips, or something."

Megan thought she had been talking very softly, but a second later Aunt Maggie's voice boomed out, "Absolutely not!"

A few minutes later, Aunt Maggie was putting a big kettle of soup on the stove, Alison and Keisha were counting out spoons and napkins, and Megan was getting bowls out of the cupboard and setting them around the table when Rosa and Heather came into the kitchen.

"Aunt Maggie," Rosa said. " We have some very bad news for you."

Aunt Maggie stopped what she was doing. "Oh?"

Rosa nudged Heather. "You tell her."

Heather cleared her throat once. "Maybe we should call the police."

4

How Will We Make It Through the Night?

Keisha dropped a spoon on the floor, which made Monty jump off his cushion on the floor and start barking.

"The police? Call 9-1-1. That's what you should do in an emergency," Keisha said.

Alison stopped counting. She and Megan looked at Aunt Maggie.

"What's wrong? Why do we need the police?" Aunt Maggie asked Heather, not sounding very worried at all.

Heather started, "It looks like someone broke into your house and stole your television…"

"And your VCR and DVD players. Even your computer is gone!" Rosa interrupted.

Aunt Maggie did one of her funny nose snorts

and then started to laugh and laugh. Monty started to bark and bark at her laughing.

"Is your aunt having a nervous breakdown?" Keisha whispered to Megan.

Then Megan started to laugh and laugh, too. Her laugh was very much like Aunt Maggie's. Monty first barked at Aunt Maggie, then he ran over and barked at Megan.

"This is getting loco," said Rosa. "That's Spanish for crazy."

"Exactly," said Alison.

Aunt Maggie used the edge of her dishtowel to dry the corners of her eyes. She had a hard time catching her breath, but finally she said, "No one broke into my house. I don't own a television or a VCR or a DVD player or a computer."

"Why not?" Keisha wanted to know.

Megan patted Monty's head to stop his barking and said, "Aunt Maggie almost never watches TV. And she doesn't like computers in her house."

"That is loco, as Rosa says," Keisha said.

Alison leaned over and whispered to Keisha, "You just called Aunt Maggie crazy for real."

"Whoops!" Keisha looked apologetically at Aunt Maggie. "Sorry. My dad says I should be respectful of people who live differently from me."

"Your father sounds like a very smart man," Aunt Maggie said, stirring the soup with a wooden spoon.

"He works at a hospital. My mom does, too. She's a nurse," Keisha said. "But they can't find a cure for my big mouth," she added, with a giggle.

The girls laughed, and Aunt Maggie rolled her eyes and said in a kidding way, "It's going to be a long, long night."

"What are we going to do all night?" Rosa asked. "I always watch TV or play computer games."

"Then tonight will be a good change for you." Aunt Maggie answered. "My favorite thing to do with my time is to use my imagination. If I'm watching television then I don't get to make up a story. It's already made up for me. I don't even get to imagine what the characters look like, because they're on my TV screen."

"Why is that a bad thing?" Heather asked.

"It's not, sometimes," said Aunt Maggie. "But imagination is like a muscle. If you don't use it, it gets very weak and after a while you can't use it anymore at all."

"Hey, that happened when I broke my arm," Alison said. "I fell on some wet grass at a soccer game. It really hurt and I had to wear a cast almost until Halloween. When they took the cast off my arm was shrunk up, much skinnier than the other one because I didn't use it for two months. It's like that, right?"

Aunt Maggie said "Exactly!" just the way Alison would say it.

Alison laughed and said, "I know. I know. My Dad is always telling me to use a different word. He told me to try 'precisely' sometimes, but that word sounds like what a scientist would say."

"How do you email your friends without a computer?" Rosa asked.

"I talk to my friends, either over the phone or face to face," Aunt Maggie replied. "That way I can listen to their wonderful voices and they can see in my eyes how much I care about them. That's what I like to do."

"I couldn't live without email," Keisha said putting her hand on her forehead in a dramatic way. "I don't know how I'm going to get through tonight."

"Oh, you'll live," Aunt Maggie said. "I have wonderful books and a drawer full of board games. I have art paper and colored pencils, glue and scissors and also scrap material and needles and thread. There are lots of things to do."

Megan was thinking about how she hadn't drawn a picture for a long, long time. The last one she drew was of a horse, a beautiful Arabian horse with a black mane and tail. She remembered making up stories about the horse, which she named "Mariah," because she heard a song once about the wind being called by that name. She had daydreamed for hours about riding her horse and feeling like the wind.

"The soup is almost ready," Aunt Maggie said, interrupting Megan's thoughts. "Megan, please go downstairs and invite Mrs. Silver up for dinner, and I will telephone the Delgados to see if they will join us."

"Mrs. Silver said she didn't need anything. Are you sure I should bother her?" Megan worried Mrs. Silver might think she was a bothersome little girl.

"She may not want to come to dinner," Aunt Maggie said. "But I know that everyone likes to at least get an invitation. No one likes to feel left out."

"That's the worst," said Rosa. "One time I didn't get invited to a birthday party and I cried and cried. After that, my mama told me that I could only have a birthday party if I invited everyone in my class."

"Where will all the people eat tonight?" Heather asked Aunt Maggie. "The table isn't big enough to fit us and everybody else."

"I'm not worried about it,'" Aunt Maggie said. "Absolutely not."

Ten minutes later the small apartment was full to

the brim with noise and laughter and people talking. Mrs. Delgado had brought up homemade corn tortillas and some shredded chicken in a sauce. Katia and Luis helped their mother warm the tortillas on the stove, and set out extra bowls they had brought from their apartment. Mr. Delgado brought his guitar and sat on a stool in the corner of the kitchen, playing cheery music. Mrs. Silver was laying out on a plate what Aunt Maggie called "Mrs. Silver's Most Famous Gingersnap Cookies."

When all the food was prepared, Aunt Maggie's voice boomed out over the noise saying, "May I have your attention, please. Let's join hands in a circle for a word of thanks."

Megan hoped Aunt Maggie wouldn't ask her to say the grace because she didn't remember any dinner prayers. Her mom was always so busy they usually had dinner standing at the kitchen counter, eating whatever was the easiest to make.

Heather raised her hand like she was in school.

"Yes, dear?" Aunt Maggie asked.

"I probably won't know your prayers, because I'm Jewish," Heather said.

Mrs. Silver went over and put her hand on Heather's shoulder. "Well, I'm Jewish, too, but that doesn't mean we can't share a word of thanks with all our friends."

"I don't think any of you will know what I'm going to say, anyway," said Aunt Maggie. "I don't even know quite yet. I plan to just speak from my heart. I believe we're all blessed by being together tonight and not out in this storm."

"Truly something to be grateful for," Mrs. Silver said. "I had no idea how I was going to eat all of those gingersnaps by myself."

Mrs. Delgado laughed and said, "Not to worry, Mrs. Silver. Not with us for neighbors."

Mr. Delgado joined hands with Keisha and Mrs. Silver, then everyone else joined hands, too, and Aunt Maggie said the most wonderful words about being safe from the storm and meeting new friends and having enough food for everyone.

When she finished, everyone lined up for hot soup that had delicious buttery, crunchy croutons on top, and warm tortillas with juicy pieces of chicken rolled into each one.

The kitchen windows were steamy and dripped water on the inside, even though the outside was frosted up with snow. Some people sat at the table and some sat at the counter. Megan shared a TV tray with Aunt Maggie. Everyone had just enough room.

Mr. Delgado told stories about his days at his

store. Katia and Luis joined in since they worked there after school. Mrs. Silver talked about her mother teaching her to bake when she was little and Aunt Maggie told great stories about touring in Broadway shows and the funny things that happened on stage. The funniest one was when Aunt Maggie was on stage and the man playing her husband stepped on her long skirt and tore the back half off. Aunt Maggie said she had to face the audience for the whole rest of the show so they couldn't see her bloomers.

"Being on stage sounds very dangerous," Katia said, as she passed around the plate of gingersnaps.

Keisha said, "I wouldn't be afraid. I'd be the best actress in the world. Except for you, Aunt Maggie."

Mrs. Silver said, "Well, right now, let's see who can be the best dish washers in the world."

Everyone helped clean up while Mr. Delgado took Monty outside for a quick walk.

When they returned, Aunt Maggie dried the snow off Monty's fur and then everyone gathered together in the living room. Mr. Delgado played more songs on his guitar and Katia and Luis sang in Spanish.

Rosa leaned over to Megan and whispered, "I'm lucky. I understand what they're singing. My papa taught me these songs, too."

The music made Megan miss her mother very much. She wished she were sitting cuddled under her arm like she did sometimes at night before bed. That's always when her mom would ask her about her day or they would read a good story. Sometimes she would hug Megan tightly and say things like, "it won't always be like this." Megan wasn't sure if her mother was talking about her job or possibly getting married again, or maybe about Megan growing up and being too big to fit under her mom's arm. Once in a while her face would look sad and she would kiss Megan on top of her head.

At those times Megan would try to remember something funny—like when she wrote "perspire" instead of "persist" in a book report. "I wrote, 'The character shows she can perspire to the end,'" she told her mother. Something like this, the thought of a character sweating and sweating until the end, would always make her mom laugh. Megan thought her mom looked like a beauty queen when she smiled. She wondered if her mother was missing her, too.

Heather was sitting on the window bench directly across from Megan and the two of them exchanged a look. Heather's eyes were almost spilling over with tears and Megan thought she was probably missing her mother, too.

Alison was sitting on the floor swaying to the music and Keisha was trying to sing along, very loudly. Finally, Mrs. Silver tapped Keisha on the back and said, "I don't think you know the words, dear."

Keisha just smiled and then shrugged. She didn't seem one bit embarrassed. Megan wished she could have that kind of confidence. Sometimes it seemed like she worried about every little thing.

Rosa was sitting on the floor in front of Mrs. Delgado, who was braiding Rosa's waist-long hair. Rosa's eyes were half-closed, as though she was dozing.

Aunt Maggie was in the rocking chair, smiling and munching on a gingersnap. At the end of one song, she said, "Perhaps I'll get out my cello and play my newest number for you."

All of a sudden Mrs. Silver shot straight up out of her chair. She held her watch up close to her eyes. "Look at the time," she said, very energetically. "I should be getting downstairs."

Megan looked at Mrs. Silver, astonished at how fast she had jumped up.

Then Mr. Delgado started to put his guitar away in its case. "Yes, yes. Mrs. Silver is right," he said. "We should go, too. I have to get up early to open the store. I'm sure many people will need bread and milk and buckets of coarse salt to melt the snow on their walks."

Luis and Katia went into the kitchen to collect their clean bowls and pans.

Mrs. Delgado hugged each of the girls goodbye, and Mrs. Silver touched them each on the cheek and said, "Be good girls."

"Goodnight, then," said Aunt Maggie. If she was disappointed about not playing her cello, she didn't show it, Megan noticed. But then, she reminded herself again, Aunt Maggie was a great actress.

Aunt Maggie bent down to kiss everyone goodbye,

even Mr. Delgado, who was nowhere near her height.

At the front door, Katia asked Aunt Maggie, 'Are you going to show the girls the attic?"

"What attic?" Keisha asked.

Heather asked Megan, "What's in the attic?"

Megan shrugged. She had never been to the attic.

Luis said, "Yes, you must show them. It's the best place on earth."

"Well, I don't know about that," Aunt Maggie said, jangling her keys in her pocket.

Katia bent her knees so she was at face level with the girls. "When Luis and I were your age we would play in the attic," she whispered. "We had the most wonderful adventures. Maybe you will, too."

"Do you still have the key?" Luis asked Aunt Maggie.

"Right here on my key ring," Aunt Maggie answered, holding it up. "It's all ready for some new explorers to take an adventure."

Megan looked closely at the key. It was the same old-fashioned golden one she had noticed earlier.

"You told us before that you would show us what the key goes to," she reminded Aunt Maggie.

"So I did," Aunt Maggie agreed.

5

Cut To . . . A Lot of Blood

After Katia and Luis left Aunt Maggie told the girls to wash up for bed. They followed her down the hallway, where she opened a little cupboard near the bathroom. On one of the shelves were lots of toothbrushes wrapped in cellophane and many little bottles of lotion and shampoo. There were also dozens of little boxes with plastic shower caps and little bars of soap and a whole cup full of tiny nail files and plastic combs. "Now no one has an excuse for not brushing your teeth and scrubbing your hands and faces. You may each take a comb, but please try not to shed too much," Aunt Maggie said.

"This is like a miniature store," Rosa remarked.

"She collects these from all the hotels she stays in when she's doing shows on the road," Megan told the other girls. When Megan was smaller she thought they were great gifts her Aunt Maggie would bring her. They were all a perfect size for smaller hands.

"I love this," said Alison. "At home I have to share a bathroom with my older brother, Mark, and my little brothers, too. I can never find my comb. The other day I caught Jason, one of the twins, using my toothbrush."

"Ew!" Megan said, grimacing. "That's disgusting."

Rosa laughed and said, "See! Don't be so sure you want a brother or sister. You've got it good, girl."

Maybe I do, Megan thought, but it would still be fun to have a little baby around. And, babies don't grow teeth for at least awhile, so she wouldn't really have to worry about having her toothbrush used right away.

Each of the girls helped themselves to some supplies and started to take turns in the bathroom. Aunt Maggie passed out tee shirts with names of famous Broadway musicals on them. They were all shows that she had been in at one time or another.

"These will have to do as nightgowns for tonight," Aunt Maggie said. They were big adult sizes, so they came down to the girl's knees.

Keisha was the last one to use the bathroom because she had stayed at the cupboard to divide all the small bath products into six piles. "Just in case," Keisha said, "we are snowed in together for a month."

Megan noticed that Aunt Maggie closed her eyes again for a moment. She wondered if she was saying another prayer.

While Keisha was in the bathroom, the girls were talking in the hallway. Suddenly they heard Keisha yell, "Ow! Ow! Oh, no! "

"Aunt Maggie! Come quickly!" Megan called out in fright.

Aunt Maggie knocked on the bathroom door and said, with alarm in her voice, "Keisha, Keisha, open up the door. Are you hurt?"

"Ow!" they heard Keisha say again. "Ow!"

"Keisha, open the door so I can help you," Aunt Maggie ordered.

The girls stood near the door, too, and Alison bent down and squinted into the keyhole.

Finally Keisha said, "Promise me you won't be mad?" There was a clicking sound as the lock turned, and the door slowly opened.

Aunt Maggie was the first one in and her voice boomed out: "What in the world???"

Keisha was standing in front of the sink. She had taken off her purple striped shirt and the girls could see that her undershirt was turning bright red under her arm. It only took a second for everyone to realize that it was blood—a lot of blood.

"Sick!" Alison cried. "What happened?"

Aunt Maggie sat Keisha down on the edge of the bathtub and quickly put a towel up to where it was bleeding.

"Look at this!" Megan had found a razor on the edge of the sink.

"Did you cut yourself?" Aunt Maggie asked. "Why did you do that?"

Megan could tell from Aunt Maggie's voice that she was pretty scared about whatever had happened, but her face still looked in control.

"I found your razor in the cabinet," Keisha confessed. "I wanted to see what it would be like to be glamorous and shave under my arms. I guess because I don't have any hair under there I cut myself."

Aunt Maggie looked a little relieved. She blotted the towel under Keisha's arm and then took it away to have a look.

"All right, you're all right," she said, after she had looked closely. "It doesn't seem to be a very deep cut."

"It sure does bleed a lot," Heather remarked.

"I had a paper cut bleed all over my best dress once," Alison said. "I was helping the twins read a book. I didn't even know I had cut my finger on the page and then there were red dots all over my blue dress. My mom asked me if it happened on purpose because I hate to wear dresses."

Aunt Maggie got a bandage and first-aid gel out of the bathroom cabinet. She washed under Keisha's arm with a washcloth and dried it with the towel. She put some first-aid gel on the bandage and taped it under Keisha's arm. She did all of this without saying one word.

Megan noticed that for the first time since she'd met her, Keisha looked embarrassed.

"Aunt Maggie," Keisha said. "I shouldn't have snooped in your cabinets and used your things. I'm sorry. I know you're going to tell my dad, right?"

Aunt Maggie still didn't say anything.

The girls all felt a little uneasy because of Aunt Maggie's silence. Was she mad? Was she going to yell? Was she out of patience? Megan was thinking that sometimes it's worse when adults are quiet than when they raise their voices.

The whole room was very, very quiet when suddenly Heather started swaying back and forth and then her head started to drop forward.

"Heather!" Megan shouted, grabbing her arm.

Alison grabbed Heather's other arm.

"Her lips are all white!" Rosa said.

Then Aunt Maggie did speak, very quickly. "Move aside, girls!" She took Heather into her arms and lowered her gently to the floor. "Get a cold wash-cloth," she ordered Megan.

Aunt Maggie patted Heather's face and said "Heather" over and over.

The girls saw that Heather's eyes were not really closed, and that mostly the white parts were showing.

"She's dead!" Rosa screamed. "I almost died earlier and now Heather is dead!"

"Is she dead, Aunt Maggie?" Alison asked, biting her fingernails. Her forehead was all scrunched up with worry.

Keisha said from the edge of the bathtub, "Is this my fault, too?"

Aunt Maggie took the cold wash cloth from Megan and spoke very firmly, "Hush up, now! Heather has fainted. She's not dead. Please, hush up!"

Even Keisha kept quiet after that.

Aunt Maggie dabbed the cloth on Heather's forehead and patted her on the cheek.

After what seemed like forever and ever, Heather opened her eyes.

Aunt Maggie said to her, "It's okay, dear. It's Aunt Maggie and you'll be okay. You fainted."

"I'm sorry," Heather said right away. "I've fainted before. I'm sorry."

"Don't be silly," Aunt Maggie said. "You can't help it. Do you feel sick?"

"No, no," said Heather. "Looking at blood makes me feel like fainting. Usually I look away, but I forgot this time."

Then Heather kind of giggled. It struck her as funny that she forgot to look away from something she hates to look at.

"Don't look over here at my undershirt, then." Keisha said.

The other girls laughed a bit more.

Aunt Maggie helped Heather sit up on the floor and then said, "Let's get you some juice." Heather seemed to be fine again, but she held on around Aunt Maggie's waist as they stood up together.

"And you," Aunt Maggie said to Keisha, putting the razor up high on the top shelf, "Please rinse out your undershirt and the towel in the bathtub with cold water. I'm leaving the door open so the other girls can keep an eye on you."

"Hey," said Keisha. "I'm trustworthy."

Everyone stopped to look at her this time.

"Okay," said Keisha, "maybe my mom is right. I'm too curious for my own good."

Megan could tell that Keisha felt really, really bad, so she helped her fill the tub to rinse out the towel.

Five minutes later, the girls poked their heads around the kitchen door. Aunt Maggie was standing next to Heather, who was sitting on a stool drinking orange juice.

"Are you okay?" Alison asked Heather.

"She's fine now," Aunt Maggie said. "But I believe we've had enough excitement for one night. It's time for bed."

6

The Magic Attic

The girls felt like groaning and complaining about going to bed. They didn't, though, because they knew that almost never changes an adult's mind about bedtime.

Aunt Maggie surprised them all, however, by asking: "Before you get into bed, who would like to see the attic?"

Everyone cheered and raised their hands except for Heather.

"Why don't you want to go?" Rosa asked Heather. "It'll be fun."

Heather just shook her head. "I don't always like new places."

Aunt Maggie turned to her. "It's a very safe and cozy place to be. In fact, I was thinking you girls might like to have your slumber party there. It's where I keep all my extra blankets, sheets and pillows."

Heather looked at her new friends' faces. She could tell they were all looking forward to seeing the attic. "I'll go if everyone else does."

"We will all go," Aunt Maggie said. "It is the most wonderful room in the whole apartment."

The girls followed her into the room next to Aunt Maggie's bedroom. In it was a roll-top desk with a lamp on it, some file cabinets and more shelves with books. On the walls were photographs of Aunt Maggie and Megan's mom along with Grandma and Grandpa Carmody. There was a school picture of Megan in third grade, too. Megan grimaced and ran over and covered the photo with her hands.

"That's the worst photo of me ever!" she cried. "I look ugly."

"Let me see!" Keisha pulled Megan's hands away.

"I love that picture," Aunt Maggie said. "It's when you first got your glasses and you still had a couple of missing teeth in front. It's adorable."

At that moment, Megan knew for sure that neither her mother nor Aunt Maggie had any idea what it was like to be ten years old. She wondered if her ears had turned bright red again from the embarrassment.

"Oh," said Keisha, "that's nothing. My school picture last year was much worse than that! My bangs were sticking straight up in the air and I had a grape-juice stain on my shirt. And what I really hated was that my mouth was wide open."

"That's hard to imagine," Aunt Maggie said, with a grin.

Heather was sitting on a twin bed against the wall and asked, "We can't all sleep in this bed, can we?"

Rosa sat down next to Heather, "This is the size of my bed at home and sometimes at night both of my little sisters, Eva and Anna, want to get under the covers with me and it's really crowded."

"Hey, what's this door?" Alison asked. She was on the other side of the room, pointing to a door next to the desk. It was only a little higher than Alison's head, but it was wider than a normal door.

Aunt Maggie walked over, taking her key ring from the pocket of her skirt.

"Ah," she said. "The door to adventure. This leads to my attic."

"Why do you keep it locked?" Keisha asked.

"My attic is full of imagination," Aunt Maggie answered, "and imagination is a wonderful and powerful thing. But it should be used in the right way, to help us make our lives and other people's lives better. I keep it locked to remind myself and whoever goes into the attic about the gift of imagination and its power."

"Is it going to be scary?" Heather asked.

"Absolutely not," Aunt Maggie said. "Everything in here is powerless—until you apply your own imagination to it."

With that Aunt Maggie put the old-fashioned key into the lock of the small door and swung it wide open. The girls could see a stairway leading up into the dark.

Aunt Maggie ducked her head, went through the door and started up the steps. "Follow me, ingenues."

The girls stood perfectly still and looked at each other. Where did the steps lead? Did they dare follow Aunt Maggie?

"Who wants to go first?" Heather asked, her voice sounding shaky.

"How about you, Alison?" Keisha asked.

Alison shifted back and forth from foot to foot. "I guess I could, but…maybe Megan should, since she's Aunt Maggie's niece."

Rosa piped up quickly. "That's a good idea."

Megan took a deep breath and went through the door. "We're right behind you, Aunt Maggie."

She started up the steps, holding on to a narrow

side railing, and when she was halfway up a light came on in the attic. Megan gasped when she got to the top.

Keisha, close behind her, said, "Are you okay?"

Megan stood at the entrance to the attic, taking in the curious setting before her. The other girls caught up with her, and they all looked around in amazement.

Aunt Maggie had turned on two lamps with pink and yellow shades, which filled the attic with a warm, rosy glow that spread to its very corners.

"Wow. How cool is this?" Keisha said.

"It's a whole secret room," said Heather.

"Exactly," said Alison.

Megan wondered if her mother had ever been in this attic before. She looked up and down the long narrow room. Stacked at one end were some cardboard boxes labeled "Decorations." There was a toolbox, a carry kennel for Monty, an art easel, a box of paints and brushes, and a sewing machine on a wooden table with a matching stool. In plastic boxes under the table were rolls and rolls of brightly colored fabric. There was a pair of gold sparkly curtains that hung on a tall frame on a stand, so it looked like a stage. There was an almost full-sized tree made of papier-mache, covered with hundreds of leaves made of green tissue. It had a birdhouse hanging on it and an actual park bench under it. Next to the bench was an old-fashioned baby carriage holding two beautiful porcelain dolls. There were three delicate Chinese paper lanterns hanging from a beam in the ceiling. On the floor was an awesome thick Oriental rug.

"It's toasty warm up here," said Rosa.

"Does anyone know the reason for that?" Aunt Maggie asked.

"I do," Megan said, "It's because heat rises, so all the heat from the building sneaks up here."

"You got it," said Aunt Maggie, smiling. "Mrs. Silver probably wishes she could talk her heat into staying downstairs."

"She's got HiHo to talk to," Rosa commented. "She doesn't need to talk to the heat."

Aunt Maggie smiled at Rosa's joke. Megan thought her mom would have smiled at it, too.

At the far end of the room was a dresser with two little drawers and two big ones. On top of the dresser was a collection of glass horses of different sizes and colors, standing proudly on a large silver tray. Megan touched the tray lightly and then looked over at Aunt Maggie who winked at her. "See," said Aunt Maggie, "you inherited more than green eyes and strawberry hair from me. I named every one of those horses when I was a girl, and I still remember their names."

Megan picked up one that looked like the Arabian horse she had drawn and thought up stories about. "What did you name this one?" she asked.

"Let me have a good look," Aunt Maggie said, coming closer. She took the glass horse in her hands. "Oh, this one was a favorite. I called her Mariah."

Megan couldn't believe what she was hearing. She had never told anyone about the stories she made up in her head.

Aunt Maggie saw Megan's mouth opened in surprise. "Yes," she continued, "I thought this horse looked as fast as the wind. There's a song about the wind being called Mariah."

"Yes, I know," said Megan. Suddenly she hugged her Aunt Maggie around the waist. She knew she would always have a special bond with her.

Aunt Maggie hugged her back. "I always wanted a horse, too. Someday, when I move from the city, I think I'll get a real one."

"You still want one?" Megan asked. She only knew other young girls who wanted horses.

"Why, yes," Aunt Maggie answered. "The things you love don't change just because you get older."

Megan nodded. This made sense. After all, she

had always loved the color yellow and chocolate chip cookies, and she couldn't imagine she would ever want to stop reading stories or dreaming about horses.

"Look at this mirror," Alison said pointing to a full-length mirror with a wood-carved edge that stood by itself on the floor. The edge was covered with flecks of gold paint. "Why do you keep a mirror up here?"

"It's not just an ordinary mirror," said Aunt Maggie. "It's especially for times when I love to use my imagination."

"It looks just regular to me," said Keisha, "Just a plain old-fashioned glass mirror."

"That's what is wonderful about it," Aunt Maggie pointed out to the girls. "There's magic in the most ordinary things in life."

"Like what kind of magic?" Megan asked.

"Well, look at the palm of your hand," Aunt Maggie said.

The girls all stopped to open up their hands and look at their palms closely.

"So what?" Keisha said. "It's skin and fingers and a thumb."

"Exactly. That's all," Alison agreed.

"Maybe that's all you see," Aunt Maggie continued, "but I see what is beyond the skin. I think about the muscles that magically do what my brain tells them to do—hold a pencil or scratch my leg. I think about the cells and how they magically grow and divide to make new cells that replace the old ones. And, I think about the DNA in those cells that came from my mother and father, and from each of their parents and from their parents before them. I think about how many many generations are all in the palm of my hand. Now, it doesn't seem so ordinary, does it?"

Rosa held her palm up close to her mouth and said, "Hi, great great great grandma Garcia."

Everyone laughed. Then Megan said, "I have my dad in my hand even though he's in Brazil."

"So, you see," Aunt Maggie said. "We're never alone, even when we think we are. That's the magic of life."

Then she led the girls over to a tall wardrobe made of beautiful, polished wood. It stood on four legs, had two large doors on the front and looked as wide as Aunt Maggie's arms would be if they were stretched out as far as they would go.

"This is one of my most treasured belongings," said Aunt Maggie, "Not only is the outside special, but you must see what the wardrobe holds."

She swung open the door. Inside was the most wonderful collection of costumes the girls had ever seen. There was a long princess gown with satiny trim and a Native American dress made of buckskins and beads. There was a long velvet cape and a cheerleader's skirt and sweater.

Heather stepped forward and put her hand on some light pink netting.

"Look at this!" she said. "It's an actual ballerina tutu! How beautiful."

The costumes seemed to go on forever and ever, more than any of the girls could have counted.

On a shelf inside the wardrobe were hats of all kinds: a cowboy hat, a furry Eskimo hood, a gorgeous feather headdress and shiny tiaras with colored gems.

On the floor next to the wardrobe was a large trunk with a curved wood lid. Aunt Maggie stepped over and used both hands to gently pull the top open.

"Of course, every outfit needs accessories. I always appreciate a complete look, head to toe," she said.

The girls knelt down around the trunk and saw shoes for any outfit a person could think of: firefighter boots, golden shoes with high heels, furry slippers, Grecian sandals that tied up the legs and ballerina slippers.

"Look at these ice skates!" Alison said, holding up a pair of gleaming blades on white leather boots. "Where did these come from?"

Aunt Maggie smiled at Alison, but Megan noticed that her eyes looked a little sad.

"Everything in the wardrobe and trunk is either a costume I wore at one time in my life or a special piece given to me by another actor. A few of the things I found at second-hand stores," Aunt Maggie said. "Each piece of clothing meant something to someone. For instance, I often use my imagination to picture who wore these firefighter boots. Was it a brave woman or man? Did they wear these in their rookie year as a firefighter?"

"I get it," said Heather. "Then you can make up a story about the boots."

"That's right," said Aunt Maggie. "Whatever story you want. Isn't that wonderful?"

"Can we look some more, Aunt Maggie?" Megan asked.

"I'll leave you girls to have some fun," Aunt Maggie said reaching deep into the wardrobe and pulling out a long piece of yellow yarn. She seemed to know just where to reach to find the yarn. She took the attic key off her key ring and threaded it on to the long piece of yarn. Then she knotted the two ends together.

"I'll trust you to be the keeper of the key, Megan," Aunt Maggie said, and put the key on the yarn over Megan's head like a necklace.

7

Key to the Past

*M*egan held the key in her hands. She felt proud that Aunt Maggie would give her the responsibility of taking care of her favorite place.

"Now," said Aunt Maggie opening the bottom drawer of the dresser and taking out a stack of blankets and sheets, "here is some bedding. The rug should be a comfortable cushion. I'll leave a nightlight on downstairs, but please be careful not to trip down the steps. I must get my beauty sleep, eight full hours, or I look like a tired Basset Hound."

"I think you're pretty, Aunt Maggie." Rosa said pulling a feather boa out of the trunk and wrapping it around her shoulders, "like a model."

"Models know how to make clothing look attractive. But true beauty comes from a woman's heart. You each seem to have a good heart, which means that you'll all be radiant women." Aunt Maggie said.

"Even if you wear glasses to read?" Megan asked.

"Yes," Aunt Maggie answered.

"Or if you feel too shy to even talk sometimes?" Heather wanted to know.

"Absolutely," Aunt Maggie replied.

"What if your bangs stick up crazy and you have grape juice on your shirt?" Keisha asked.

Aunt Maggie laughed. "True beauty even shines through a bad hair day. Isn't that wonderful to know? Good night, ingenues."

"Good night," called the girls as Aunt Maggie went down the steps.

Megan and Heather started to spread the blankets and sheets on the Oriental rug to make beds. Rosa, Keisha and Alison couldn't pull themselves away from the wardrobe and the trunk.

"Look," said Rosa, holding up a long grass skirt in front of her at the mirror. "It's a Hawaiian skirt, like the dancers wear." Rosa looked like she had an idea and disappeared behind the shiny gold curtains. A moment later she pushed the curtains apart dramatically and made an entrance. She was wearing the grass skirt and swinging her hips from side to side. She even twirled her

hands in the air in the way a Hawaiian dancer would.

Megan and Heather clapped.

"Now all we need is some pineapple," Megan said.

"And a sandy beach," Heather added.

"Check me out," Keisha said. She had pulled on a cheerleading skirt and had also found big, puffy pompoms. She jumped up in the air, holding the pompoms above her head and did a cheer.

"I've got spirit, yes, I do, I've got spirit! How about you?"

Megan cheered back. "You go, girl!"

Rosa said, "You'd be a good cheerleader, Keisha."

"I'm going to try out for the squad at my school for the spring sports." Keisha announced.

"I could never do that," Heather said. "I'd freak out with bleachers full of people looking at me."

"Ooooh, I can't wait," Keisha said. "I'll cheer people right out of their seats."

Alison wasn't making much noise at all. She was completely captivated by a lavender-colored ice skating dress she had found in the wardrobe. She turned the hanger in her hands so the girls could see all sides of the costume. "This must have been worn at a world championship event. It's totally pro, I can tell."

"That's my favorite color," Keisha said, adjusting

the purple scrunchie that held up some of her long black hair, "as you can probably tell. It would be pretty with your blonde hair, Alison."

"And look," Megan said, kneeling at the trunk. "Here's a pair of tights that match perfectly."

"I love all the beads on it." Rosa added. "That must have taken forever to make. I made beaded necklaces to sell at our church fundraiser and each one took me hours."

"Oh! Did you see this silver tiara?" Heather asked looking on the shelf of the wardrobe. "This has to go with it. Try it on, Alison."

"This would be like the best birthday wish ever coming true," Alison said softly as Heather placed the tiara on top of her head. "I'd love to be spinning around in the center of an ice rink with a spotlight on me. I watch all the ice skating programs I can and I'm taking lessons at the rink near my house."

"I knew you must be good at skating," Megan said, "especially since you have your own pair."

"I wanted to show everyone today how I can do a waltz jump on skates," Alison said. "I always practice because I want to be the best skater in my age group."

"Is a figure skater what you want to be when you grow up?" Heather asked her.

"Exactly," Alison answered and then added, "or a professional soccer player, or a gymnast, or a basketball player, or the first girl quarterback in the NFL."

Megan laughed and said, "Maybe you should just say 'something to do with sports'."

The other girls all said at almost the same time, "Exactly."

After the costumes were put back the girls slipped between the covers and fluffed their pillows.

"What do you want to be, Megan?" Keisha asked.

"Hmm." Megan thought. "Maybe a horse trainer or a foreign corespondent, like my Dad."

"I want to be a news announcer, " Rosa said, "so I can be the first one to tell everyone what is happening. I think I'd be good at interviews because I can speak both Spanish and English. Or maybe a fashion designer, so I could make really cool clothes."

"That's great," said Heather. "What I'd love to be is a ballerina, so I could dance all day long. If I were a ballerina, you could design a costume for me."

"I could see you being a ballerina," said Rosa. "You have really long legs. Mine are short. I'll probably have to stand on a stool to interview people!"

"Keisha, what about you? You didn't tell us what you want to be," Megan asked.

"I've been thinking," Keisha said, sitting up. "I can see myself as the first Black woman president of the United States, or, maybe the most famous pop singer in the world. Or I might turn out to be the first woman to build an apartment complex on the moon."

The girls all started to giggle.

"I want to be the biggest thing ever!" Keisha said. "I just have to figure out what that is. But I'll have to tell you tomorrow because I'm too tired to think anymore."

She flopped back on her pillow and pulled a blanket up to her chin.

"Me, too." Heather yawned. "It must be late."

Heather's yawn became contagious and one by one the girls each yawned and snuggled into their blankets on the soft rug.

Heather, Rosa and Keisha all closed their eyes and seemed to soon be asleep. Megan closed hers, too, but she didn't fall asleep right away. When she opened her eyes, she noticed that Alison was standing in front of the mirror, holding the skating dress up to her. She crawled out from under the covers to stand next to her.

"I couldn't stop thinking about this skating dress," Alison whispered. "I can just see myself twirling and jumping in it. So I had to take one more look at it."

"It must be great to be athletic," whispered back

Megan. "I can't even stand up straight on skates."

"Maybe you haven't had a chance to practice."

"The truth is, I'm kind of scared of getting hurt," Megan said. "That's probably why I like books. You can either read or you can't. You don't have to compete."

"Competition is fun," Alison replied. "It makes you want to do the best you can. You have to have confidence in yourself for any sport."

Megan took the key from around her neck and dangled it near her eyes and said, "Maybe it could happen if I could imagine it."

Alison stepped behind Megan at the mirror and held the skating dress up in front of her. "Okay. Just imagine yourself as an ice skater, going faster and faster across the ice rink."

The two girls looked into the mirror. Suddenly there were two flashes of light across the attic ceiling, like two shooting stars in the sky. Alison and Megan both closed their eyes against the brightness.

"What was that?" Keisha asked, sitting up on her blanket. Rosa and Heather rubbed their eyes as three more flashes of light crossed the attic.

When the girls opened their eyes again they were no longer in Aunt Maggie's attic and they weren't even all together anymore.

8

Groovy Place, But Where are We?

Megan felt herself moving very, very fast but she could tell she wasn't running or even walking. When she looked down to see what her feet were doing she saw that she was wearing the lavender skating dress and was zooming across a rink in a new pair of skates. How can this be happening? Megan thought. I never really learned how to skate. But for some reason Megan's feet seemed to know exactly what to do.

"You're looking really good out there, Megan," a woman called from the edge of the rink.

"Thanks," said Megan, taking a moment to glance over at the woman. She had blonde curly hair and was wearing a warm-up suit with a shiny satin jacket over it.

"Now let's see your final loop jump," the woman encouraged Megan.

"Okay," Megan heard herself answer. Her heart was beating so fast she was sure the woman could see how nervous she was. Was this really happening? Megan expected to wipe out at any second and go sprawling across the ice. But she didn't.

Instead, Megan's body turned on the ice to do backward crossovers. Then, picking up speed again, she felt herself bend deeply and push up high into the air. She pulled her arms in close to her body and then opened them again right before she landed. Somehow she landed on her right foot, bent at the knee, and glided gently backward.

Megan was so excited about her skating ability she threw her arms up in the air in victory.

"Bravo," called the woman at the sidelines. "That was a perfect loop jump. Now, come off the ice. I've got good news for you."

Megan skated towards the woman because she didn't know what else to do. She had no idea where she was. The woman put her hand on Megan's shoulder as she stepped off the ice and said, "Great improvement. That was really outta sight!"

Out of sight? Megan glanced at the woman's face

to see if she was laughing. She had read that word in books, but she hadn't ever heard anybody use it.

Then Megan noticed the woman's shiny jacket had the name Elaine Locke stitched on it over the pocket. She was holding a clipboard with a list of skating moves on it. Megan could see her name and the terms choctaw, crossover and toe loop, with a check mark next to each word. Megan decided she must be a coach.

"Megan, you're acting rather strange today," Coach Locke said seriously as Megan walked by her on her skates.

Megan's face went pale with fear. She was certain that the coach had figured out that she had no business being there, wherever it was.

"You know you should always put guards on your blades anytime you're off the ice." Coach Locke said, handing Megan two plastic protectors for her skates.

Megan breathed a sigh of relief and said, "Sorry, Coach Locke. I think I got too excited."

Coach Locke said, "Well, I don't blame you. Especially since you and Alison both passed another Figure Skating Association test and are getting closer to competing professionally."

"I did?" Megan shrieked with joy. "We did?"

Suddenly someone else was hugging her tightly

and jumping up and down with excitement. It was Alison, who must have been sitting on a bench with about ten other girls, all of them wearing skates.

Megan hugged Alison back and whispered, "I'm so glad you're here with me, but where are we?"

Alison leaned in towards Megan's ear. "Maybe it's a dream, but is it my dream or yours?"

Megan shook her head. "I don't know. Do you think the other girls are here, too?"

Alison said quietly, "While you were on the ice I tried to look around. I didn't see them, but there's a banner over our heads that might be the answer to where we are."

"All right, you two," Coach Locke said. "Let's join the group and get ready for ballet lessons."

The other girls on the bench congratulated Megan and Alison as they gathered up their gear. Megan looked up at the banner as she pulled on the only sweater left, a yellow one. She figured it must be hers.

The banner read: "Colorado Springs Training for the 1976 Olympics."

That's a long time ago, Megan thought, 1976 was way before she was born. Could they possibly be that far back in time?

Alison leaned over to Megan again and said, "I

think 1976 is a couple of years away because coach was saying that by the time the Olympics roll around Jenny should be their best hope for a gold medal."

"Jenny who?" Megan asked.

"Taylor, I think," Alison answered. "She was my mom's favorite skater when she was my age. In fact, I have a picture of my mom with a Jenny Taylor haircut. They called it a 'wedge'."

One of the girls who had been sitting on the bench approached Alison and Megan. Over her pink practice dress, she wore a white sweater with a fur collar. Her light-brown hair was done in two long braids with white satin ribbons woven into them. Her nose turned up at the end, and looked like a little button in the middle of her face. She was wearing very pink lip gloss, too.

"Her name is Debbie," Alison whispered to Megan. "I heard someone talking to her earlier."

"Far out!" Debbie said to Megan, with a smile that did not seem very sincere. "It's really neat that you both passed. I'm going to try next week. I know I'll pass. My mother was a professional skater and she told me I'm already better than everyone in this group."

"Well, good luck, Debbie," Megan answered carefully, not sure how else to respond.

"Wouldn't it be groovy if Coach Locke let us

watch the seniors skate for a little while instead of going straight to ballet class?" Debbie said, loud enough for Coach Locke to hear.

Coach Locke turned to Debbie and said, "All right. You can all stay and watch the senior skaters rehearse this morning, but I'm going to have the junior ballet instructor come down here and work on arm movement with all of you in the meantime."

The girls on the bench all cheered and Alison shouted out, "Solid, Coach Locke, solid."

"Solid?" Megan asked, raising her eyebrows at Alison.

"I'm trying to fit in," Alison said under her breath, with a little giggle.

Megan had put a couple of more pieces into the puzzle of where they were, but she had no idea how they got there or how she was ever going to fit in. She remembered reading in a schoolbook that Colorado Springs was known as a professional skater's training ground.

She knew that some young girls often leave their families and live with coaches to be able to train for at least four or five hours a day. Megan wondered if she and Alison were staying with their coach.

Just then Coach Locke reappeared with the junior

ballet instructor. Both Megan and Alison gasped out loud when they saw her. The instructor was Heather.

Heather was wearing a dance leotard and skirt, and ballet slippers. Her hair was pulled back into a bun. She saw Alison and Megan and almost started to run towards them, clearly relieved to know she wasn't alone.

Megan grabbed Heather's hand and Alison whispered, "Have you seen Keisha or Rosa?" Heather started to answer, when Coach Locke took her arm and led her in front of the group.

Coach Locke said to the group of girls, "Pay attention to Heather, please. The judges always look for artistic interpretation on the ice, so this is important."

Heather opened her mouth to say something to the coach, but nothing came out.

The coach didn't seem to notice as she patted Heather on the back and said, "Take over."

Heather began to lift her arms, as though she had no idea what she was doing. She looked like she could burst into tears. But as she put her arms up over her head, she took on the air of a confident and beautiful young ballerina.

She took the girls through graceful sweeping arm motions with her neck stretched long, her back perfectly straight and her head held high. Once she realized she knew what she was doing, Heather had a look of confidence on her face that Megan and Alison couldn't believe. Was this the same Heather who could barely speak?

Heather walked through the group smiling and gently coaching each of the girls on their posture. She congratulated the ones who held the pose well, and encouraged the girls who were having a harder time.

When she walked between Megan and Alison she whispered, "Is this really me? It's so exciting. I'm a true dancer."

"And a dyn-o-mite one," Alison giggled.

"Far out!" Megan said, grinning at her groovy new language.

"Please clear the ice! I've got a job to do!" A clear loud voice rang out. Megan, Heather and Alison looked at each other as the last skaters on the ice scattered to the edges. Could it possibly be true?

9

Something Went Terribly Wrong

On the ice, sitting high up in a large box-shaped machine was Keisha. She was steering the machine around the rink in a perfect pattern. Every place she drove, the ice became smooth like wet glass. An older man wearing coveralls and a wool cap was riding with Keisha. He looked a little nervous, but told her she was doing a pretty good job.

"Thanks, Arthur," Keisha said. "You're not bad at driving the Macaroni either."

"That's Zamboni!" the girls could hear Arthur telling Keisha as he shook his head.

"Right," said Keisha. "Zamboni. I never thought the first thing I learned to drive would be a Zamboni."

Suddenly, Keisha caught sight of Megan, Heather and Alison.

"Up here!" she shouted down to them. "I thought I was by myself. I'm so happy to see you guys. I don't know why, but I'm smoothing over the ice with this huge machine! "

Alison leaned towards Megan and said, "She did say she wanted to be the biggest thing there is. Right? And that Zamboni is the biggest thing here."

Megan giggled and waved up to Keisha, who called out, "Guess who's going to skate in the seniors practice next?"

Megan almost took a guess, but Keisha shouted the answer down before anyone could respond.

"Jenny! Can you believe it? My mom was nine when she won the gold medal!"

Arthur looked over at her like she was crazy, because of course that hadn't happened yet, and it didn't make sense that Keisha's mother could be only nine years old.

Keisha realized her mistake, and smiled and shrugged at Arthur. "I just mean it would be a bummer if she didn't win one. You know…sometime."

Keisha made a motion to the other girls like she was going to zip her mouth shut and then she steered the machine around in another big circle.

Megan called up to Keisha, "You go, girl!"

"Where do you want her to go? She has to clean the ice," Debbie asked, stepping out of the group of girls and walking up to Megan, "You know that Zamboni girl? She's a head trip."

Megan didn't know what that meant, but it sounded insulting.

"Keisha's totally awesome…uh, I mean groovy." Megan said to Debbie.

"Right on," said Alison. "Keisha's boss."

"That's right. Keish is hip," Heather joined in.

"Hip?" Debbie repeated.

Alison whispered to Heather, "I think hip is from the '90s."

"Oh," said Heather. "I better stick to ballet."

Debbie looked at the rest of the girls and said, loudly enough for them to all hear, "If you ask me, you're all weirdoes. You may have passed the skating test today, but you'll never be as neat as Jenny." Some of the other girls laughed and started to gather around Debbie.

The Zamboni made its last turn and Keisha drove it off the ice, waving to her friends.

"I wonder where Rosa is," Megan said, just loud enough for Alison and Heather to hear.

Heather answered, "I hope she isn't lost again.

I've tried looking for her, but she must be someplace we haven't thought of."

Alison leaned into the conversation. "She must be here somewhere. It's too bad she's missing all the excitement."

Megan searched the circumference of the ice arena looking for any sign of Rosa. On the other side, near the dressing room entrance, Megan could see four young women doing stretching exercises. One in particular caught her eye. She was very tall and wore wire-rim glasses. Her strawberry-blonde hair was pulled back in a bun. There was something familiar about her.

"Who's that girl?" Megan, pointing, dared to ask Coach Locke when she joined the group again to watch the seniors.

"That's Margaret," Coach Locke told Megan. "She's such a sweet girl, with a big heart. Unfortunately, she's grown too tall and awkward for figure skating. It's just easier for girls who weigh less to make good jumps."

"That's too bad," Megan said.

"Well, not everyone can compete at an Olympic level. Very few make it. It's the risk you take getting into this sport," the coach said. "You should keep your eye on Jenny today. She's going to skate third, right after Juli and Janet. She's very graceful, which is what

I'm trying to teach you girls now."

Then the lights in the skating rink went down and a voice came over the loud speaker. "Ladies and gentlemen, welcome to the Colorado Springs Ice Arena."

Alison grabbed Megan. "Rosa! That has to be Rosa's voice!"

"Of course," Heather said. "That's right. She did say she wanted to be an announcer."

Megan looked up into the balcony at the enclosed box seats where the light and sound operators and the commentators were stationed. There was Rosa, at a table with a microphone.

"This morning's practice session is a rehearsal for tonight's showcase performance. Each skater will have ice time to rehearse their complete free-style program. Names were picked out of a hat to determine the order of performance. First Juli will skate, then Janet, then Jenny and last will be Margaret. Can we have the first skater take the ice, please."

Keisha gave Rosa a thumbs-up from the top of the Zamboni. Rosa had a confused smile on her face as she shrugged and mouthed the words, "Where are we?"

Keisha pointed at Alison, Megan and Heather. When Rosa saw them, she began to wave enthusiastically. The girls waved back. There was something comforting in knowing they were all sharing the same experience.

Alison, Megan, Heather and the other girls stood along the wall at the edge of the rink to watch with Coach Locke. Both Juli and Janet skated beautifully to their music, doing very difficult moves with a lot of style. It was easy to see why they were already junior champions.

Then Jenny took to the ice. She looked very nervous at the start, but once the music was playing her skating became almost magical. It didn't even look like hard work from where the girls watched. She leapt into her jumps, seeming to hang in the air for endless moments. For the final move of her routine, she performed a beautiful spin that she had created on her own. It was obvious that Jenny was a skating star.

When she finished, all the girls and everyone else watching cheered and cheered.

Debbie said out loud, "I'm sure I'll be Jenny's good friend. She's such a perfect skater and that's what I'm going to be, too."

Coach Locke said, "Practice, practice and more practice."

"I know, Coach. I know!" Debbie said in a very cranky tone of voice, flipping one of her braids over her shoulder and hitting Megan in the eye.

"Ouch," Megan put her hand up to her eye.

"Are you going to start crying?" Debbie asked very sarcastically.

Megan wished she could think of something to say back to her like, "Nice braids, Pocahontas," but she couldn't get up the courage.

Alison saw what happened and came over. She pointed at Debbie's neck and let out a scream. It even startled Megan.

"What? What's the matter?" Debbie asked, looking very scared.

"It looks like there's something biting your neck!" Alison pointed and shrieked.

Debbie started jumping up and down and shaking her head and neck around. She was shouting, "Get it off! Get it off!"

Then Alison said, "Oh, sorry. It's just the fur collar on your sweater. Never mind."

Megan put her hand over her mouth to stop a giggle. She noticed that even Coach Locke had to turn her face away because she was smiling.

Debbie looked steaming mad and said to some of the other girls, "Let's go. Who cares about watching Margaret skate? She'll never make it and she's the only one left."

Coach Locke took Debbie by the shoulder and said, "You'll stay and watch Margaret because she deserves that respect. She's an advanced skater."

Debbie said, sulkily, "Okay, I'll stay. But, she doesn't have a chance to ever compete in the Olympics, does she, Coach?"

Coach Locke looked a little bit sad and said, "Maybe not. But I think Margaret is going to be a great woman someday, no matter what she does."

Megan watched as Margaret skated out into the middle of the rink and froze in a beginning pose waiting for her music to start. The music was sad and sweet and Margaret's face showed all the emotion of each note.

About two minutes into the routine, she performed a double toe loop and stumbled, just a bit, at the landing.

"See what I mean?" Debbie said with a sneer. "She can't even do it right in practice. How will she ever compete?"

Alison bit her lip in anger at Debbie's mean words.

"Her style in her arm movements is beautiful," Heather said out loud.

"Yes, it is," Coach Locke replied. "If only her legs had that same coordination."

Then Margaret tried a difficult jump. She took off in a forward position, starting out with good form, and got quite high in the air. Then something went terribly wrong.

While she was up in the air the blade of her right skate hooked with the blade of her left skate, making it impossible to separate her feet for the landing.

Coach Locke gasped. "Oh, no!"

"What a klutz!" Debbie laughed, until she saw what happened next.

10

True Champion

Margaret landed on the side of her lower leg and crashed to the ice. Her glasses flew off her face and slid across the rink. Then she let out a horrible scream.

Coach Locke hurried out onto the ice and so did some of the girls, but the first one at Margaret's side was Jenny.

She knelt down next to Margaret on the ice and took off her warm-up jacket to make a pillow for Margaret's head. Then she looked up at Coach Locke and said, "I think Margaret has hurt her leg pretty bad."

Everyone could see why Jenny thought so when they were close enough to see what had happened. Margaret's leg was already swollen and the skin was purple and black near the top of her skate boot.

Rosa's voice came over the speaker system. "I will call for an ambulance."

Coach Locke looked up and nodded at Rosa.

Margaret was crying and saying, "My leg. It hurts so badly. What happened?"

Margaret tried to sit up to see what happened to her leg, but Jenny gently held her down on the ice.

Jenny stroked Margaret's hair and said, "Help is coming. You'll be okay. I'm right here."

Margaret put her head in Jenny's lap and cried some more.

"Oh, Jenny," she said. "What am I going to do?"

Alison and Megan looked at Jenny's face. She looked like she could start crying, too.

Keisha came up behind Jenny. She had picked Margaret's glasses up from the ice and now she handed them to Jenny.

Megan took off her sweater and lay it over Margaret to help keep her warm. Even though she didn't know her at all, she took Margaret's hand and held it.

Moments later Rosa's voice came over the speaker again. "Please clear a path. The ambulance will arrive at any minute."

Everyone who was surrounding Margaret except for Jenny and Megan stepped back to let the paramedics through. Soon Margaret was placed on a stretcher and was being wheeled toward the door of the ambulance.

"I'll follow behind the ambulance in my car, Margaret," Coach Locke said. "Don't be afraid."

"She won't be afraid, because I'm going with her," Jenny said.

"But what about your preparation for tonight's show? Don't you need to practice your routine again?" Coach asked Jenny.

"Don't you want your hair and makeup done?" Debbie asked. "You won't have time if you go to the hospital with Margaret."

Jenny stopped and looked at everyone. "My friend Margaret is more important to me," she said. "She needs me and I'm going to go with her."

The paramedics nodded when Jenny asked if she could ride in the back of the ambulance.

Before the doors shut, Jenny said to Megan, "Will you please pick up my gear and Margaret's gear and keep it safe for us until tonight?"

Megan nodded. "Of course. I'll find you later."

Debbie pushed Megan aside. "I'll take care of your stuff, Jenny."

Jenny shook her head no. "Thanks, anyway, I've already asked Megan," she said.

As the ambulance drove off with the sirens blaring, Coach Locke addressed the group of girls.

"The difference between a great skater and a true champion is that a true champion always has a great heart. What you've seen today is a true champion. Don't ever forget it."

Later in the day, as the girls were working on schoolwork with a tutor provided for the skaters, Rosa made another announcement over the loud speaker.

"I know you are all very worried about Margaret. Jenny just called from the hospital. Margaret did break her leg but the doctors were able to set it and put it in a cast. She's going to be able to go home today."

Alison and Megan looked at each other with relief in their eyes. They had felt so badly for Margaret.

Rosa made another announcement. "Tonight's showcase will go on as planned, with two changes."

Debbie dropped her pencil onto her paper and announced to the other girls: "Well, I'm the most special skater in this group, so maybe I'll be asked to do a performance."

Coach Locke suddenly appeared in the doorway. "There will be a special performance tonight," she said, "but it won't be by you, Debbie. I'm sorry if you're disappointed."

Many of the girls looked at each other with anticipation.

"The senior coach, Mr. Sumner, was watching our test session earlier and has asked that Alison McCann perform a short program tonight."

"Me?" Alison asked in disbelief.

"Her?" Debbie asked, turning her nose even higher up into the air.

"Congratulations, Alison," Megan said. "You're a great competitor."

Coach Locke said to Alison, "Come with me and we'll pick out some music and work on your routine. It doesn't have to be perfect. Everyone knows you are doing this at the last minute."

Alison gathered up her books, winked at Megan and said, "Far out!"

"Right on!" Megan replied, winking back.

Before the coach left she said to Megan, "Megan, Jenny would like you to come to her dressing room before the show. She has something to share with you."

"Me?" Megan asked excitedly.

"Her?" Debbie said, rolling her eyes in disgust. "Wait until my mother hears this."

Coach Locke looked over at her. "Debbie, you have a lot of talent," she said quietly. "But you can't expect to have what you want without working hard. Your mother isn't going to always be able to make everything go your way. Success can't be coaxed or bought. You have to work for it."

"I know, Coach, I know," Debbie said, in a surprisingly subdued voice. And instead of flipping her braids this time, she nodded her head with understanding.

That evening, as the crowd filled in all of the seats in the arena, Keisha drove the Zamboni around the ice to smooth over any scratches that had been made during the practice sessions. Her face looked very serious; you could see she didn't want to miss a single patch. She only had a moment for a quick wave at Heather, who was leading Juli and Janet in some stretching exercises, and one for Alison, waiting at the edge of the rink.

After leaving Jenny's dressing room, Megan found Alison. She had given her the beautiful lavender skating dress to wear in the show. The sheer sleeves were the perfect length on Alison, and the beads on the front seemed to catch the sparkle in her eyes. The best part was the shiny tiara on her head.

"You're going to be great." Megan hugged her.

"Just don't tell me to 'break a leg,'" Alison laughed. "I'm so psyched!"

"Shhh," Megan said. "No one's going to know

what psyched means. They might think you're having a breakdown or something."

"Exactly," Alison said. Both of the girls giggled.

"Why did Jenny want to see you?" asked Alison.

"It's a surprise," said Megan. "You'll find out later. Just concentrate on doing the best you can."

Megan could hear the crowd's excitement as the lights dropped down lower. She looked up to the announcer's booth to watch Rosa introduce the show. First Rosa told the crowd about the changes in the program because of Margaret's accident.

The crowd groaned, until Rosa said, "As a special treat, we'd like to introduce an up-and-coming skater with a lot of promise. She's only ten years old, but if she continues to fulfill her tremendous potential in the years to come, we have no doubt she'll become a champion skater. Please welcome Alison McCann."

Alison skated into the center of the ice in the dark and took a pose. The music started up, and seemed to carry Alison's body through the entire two-minute program. The crowd burst into applause as Alison performed a double toe loop and then a lutz. She glided around the ice, using the arm moves Heather had taught her earlier, and ended the program with an almost perfect layback spin. She arched her back so far it almost touched the skate raised up behind her. When she finished, her face was flushed pink with excitement and the crowd was on its feet, cheering on a new star.

Alison looked over at Megan who was standing with Juli, Janet and Jenny. They were cheering wildly.

Alison curtsied deeply to each end of the arena, and then to the sides. She skated over to Coach Locke, who was waiting with a warm hug. Even Debbie reached over to pat Alison on the back.

Juli's and Janet's performances also met with the crowd's enthusiastic approval. Then Rosa's voice filled the arena again.

Rosa said, "Jenny Taylor has asked me to announce a surprise. Even though her good friend Margaret's accident prevents her from skating tonight, Jenny has asked her to perform. Before practice this morning, Margaret shared a poem that is one of her personal favorites with Jenny. Jenny feels the poem represents the true spirit of skating, with all of its ups and downs, and the unknown experiences that each of our futures hold. She has asked Margaret to share the poem with all of you. Please welcome Margaret Carmody."

11

So That Explains It

The spotlight shone on Margaret. She was in a wheelchair with her leg in a cast suspended on a support in front of her. The crowd applauded and cheered.

"Carmody?" Megan asked as she prepared to push Margaret's wheelchair out onto the rink.

"Yes, that's my name. Margaret Carmody. But my family calls me Maggie."

Megan turned to look at Alison, Keisha and Heather to see if they realized what was being revealed. They all looked just as surprised as Megan, and Keisha mouthed the words: "Aunt Maggie!"

Megan, both nervous at being in the spotlight and excited by this discovery, wondered if the crowd could see her knees shaking as she pushed the wheelchair onto the ice. The spotlight followed Megan and Margaret to the center of the rink, where Rosa was waiting to hand Margaret a microphone on a long chord.

"Thank you," said Margaret. "I'd like to read a poem, which some of you may recognize as a song by one of my favorite music groups. It's called "Ripple.""

Margaret began to read. Even though she wasn't singing, the words sounded like music floating above the ice and filling the arena. The audience listened so quietly that it almost seemed like Margaret was the only person in the enormous arena.

> If my words did glow
> With the gold of sunshine
> And my tunes were played
> On the harp unstrung,
> Would you hear my voice
> Come through the music?
> Would you hold it near,
> As it were your own?
>
> It's a hand-me-down,
> The thoughts are broken,
> Perhaps they're better
> Left unsung.
> I don't know,
> Don't really care.
> Let there be songs
> To fill the air.
>
> Ripple in still water,
> When there is no pebble tossed,
> Nor wind to blow.
>
> Reach out your hand,
> If your cup be empty,
> If your cup is full,
> May it be again.
> Let it be known
> There is a fountain
> That was not made
> By the hands of men.
>
> There is a road,
> No simple highway
> Between the dawn
> And the dark of night
> And if you go,
> No one may follow
> That path is for
> Your steps alone.

When she finished there was absolute silence for at least one minute, and then the audience began to applaud. Some people even stood up to clap.

Coach Locke skated out to hug Margaret and said, "Congratulations, I think you've found your true gift—sharing through words."

Megan hugged Margaret, too, then turned the wheelchair around and pushed it towards the edge of the ice. Jenny met them as she came on to the ice to skate her showcase routine. She bent to hug Margaret.

"Thank you, Margaret," Jenny said. "Your courage gives me courage, too."

Megan, Alison, Keisha, Rosa and Heather were all in Jenny's dressing room after the show. Margaret was having her cast signed by everyone who came by to congratulate them both on a wonderful performance.

"Hey, I'd like a little credit for such a successful show," said Keisha, with a big grin on her face. "After all, skaters always look better on silky smooth ice."

"Yes, Keisha," Jenny said. "You are the queen of Zambonis."

The girls all laughed and Alison put her skating tiara on Keisha's head.

"Zamboni queen!" Keisha said, with a smirk. "I think I like that."

Jenny had ten bouquets of flowers in her dressing room that had been tossed by fans onto the ice following her performance. Every two minutes another armful of flowers would be brought in.

"I should go out and sign autographs," Jenny said. "My fans are very kind. Margaret, why don't you come, too? I'm sure they'll want to talk to you."

"All right," Margaret said. "Then I have to go home. I've missed my mother and my father and especially my little baby sister, Julia."

"Julia's my mom!" Megan burst out in excitement.

"Uh-oh," said Alison.

The room got quiet and Margaret looked deeply into Megan's eyes. For a moment there seemed to be a true connection that only happens between family members. It was as if Megan was looking into the palm of her hand and could see the history of her family.

Then Jenny said, "Isn't it funny that your mom's name is Julia, too? You know, you both look quite a bit alike, almost as if you could be related."

Alison jumped in. "Well, we are all a big skating family, right?"

"Right on!" Rosa said.

"Outta sight!" Heather piped up.

Jenny pushed Margaret's wheelchair to the door

and then said to the girls, "Hope we see you again."

Megan said, "Thanks. I'll always remember you. I have the feeling that the whole world will, too."

After Jenny and Margaret were gone Keisha closed the door to the dressing room. "Now what?" she asked. "Will I always be a Zamboni queen?"

"I'd like to go back now," Heather said, "even though I loved being a professional dancer."

"Can we?" Rosa asked. "Is it possible to go back? "

They were all silent for a moment, wondering.

"Let's think about how we got here in the first place," Alison said, finally. "I was holding a skating dress in front of Megan."

"That's right," Megan remembered. "And we were in front of the mirror."

All five of the girls stood up together and looked into Jenny's makeup mirror.

"Nothing's happening," Keisha said. "Don't tell me I have to live in a world that hasn't invented email yet. And—oh no! There won't be any 'Action Expedition', either!"

"Don't panic," said Alison. "There must have been something else."

"The key!" Megan said, with excitement. "Remember, I was holding up the key."

"Where is it?" Heather asked.

Megan put her hand on the back of her neck. The piece of yarn was still there. She tugged on the yarn until the key appeared out of the top of her sweater.

"Here it is!" She held it up in front of the mirror.

Suddenly, five bright flashes of light, like shooting stars, filled the dressing room. All of the girls closed their eyes.

When Megan opened her eyes again she was back in her Aunt Maggie's attic, tucked into the blankets on the Oriental rug. She looked around to see Alison, Keisha, Rosa and Heather all blinking their eyes.

"I think I had a really strange dream," Keisha said.

"Me, too," said Rosa.

Heather looked at Megan. "Were we dreaming?"

Keisha sat up on the blanket and rubbed her forehead under her bangs, "All I know is I feel like I was really busy all night long."

Megan was glad to be back under the covers. She lifted her head off the pillow long enough to say to Alison, "You were right. I could skate once I had the confidence."

Alison smiled from her pillow. "Exactly," she said.

Magic Attic Club

A patch of bright sunlight on Megan's face woke her up the next morning. The light was coming through the dormer windows high up in the attic walls. Megan squinted in the sunlight. Suddenly she heard an awful noise. It woke up the other girls right away.

Rosa sat up and covered her ears. "What is that horrible noise?"

"This is torture," Keisha said, pulling her pillow over her head.

It was like nothing Megan had ever heard. It was a screeching, squawking sound, worse than nails on a chalkboard.

Heather looked afraid. "Do you think some kind of wild animal got into the house overnight?"

"I'll find out," said Alison, jumping up from her blanket.

"Wait!" said Megan. "I'll go with you."

"Hey, I'm not getting left behind again," said Rosa, joining them at the top of the stairs.

"Come on, Keisha," Heather said, pulling the pillow away from Keisha's head. "Let's go, too."

The girls went quickly down the stairs and followed the direction of the terrible sound. They walked down the hallway on tiptoes, worried about who or what they might find. The sound grew louder as they approached the living room. It was clearly coming from there.

Megan put her hands on the frame of the doorway and very slowly peeked into the room.

"Aunt Maggie!" Megan yelled, and then covered her mouth with her hand.

"Oh, no!" screamed Rosa. "Is she dead?"

Alison picked up one of the heavy awards from the hallway table and charged towards the doorway. "I'll save her!" she said, waving the award above her head.

Suddenly the terrible noise stopped. All five of the girls stood in the doorway, and looked at Aunt Maggie who was sitting on the long bench next to the bookshelves. In front of her was the music stand.

Propped up against her was a cello. In Aunt Maggie's hand was a bow, which she was dragging across the strings of the cello. Monty was on the floor at her feet. His head was down and he was covering his ears with his paws.

Aunt Maggie looked startled to see the girls.

"You shouldn't sneak up on people, ingenues," she said. "Especially when they are deep in concentration."

Megan started to snicker a bit and then Rosa caught the giggle bug. Keisha put her hand over her mouth, which made Alison and Heather burst out laughing.

"Oh, Aunt Maggie," Megan said. "We thought something terrible was happening."

"Absolutely not," said Aunt Maggie. "I'm just trying to learn to play cello. That song was 'Edelweiss' from *The Sound of Music*."

"Are you sure?" Keisha asked.

"Oh, dear," said Aunt Maggie. "Someday I'll get better, if I practice, practice, practice. But today we'll eat oatmeal instead. Come along, ingenues. I have hot cereal on the stove."

The girls followed Aunt Maggie down the hall to the kitchen. Megan watched Aunt Maggie's jaunty stride closely.

"Aunt Maggie," she asked, "are you sorry you broke your leg ice skating when you were young?"

Aunt Maggie stopped in the hallway and looked at Megan for what seemed like a long time. "How do you know that's what happened?"

Megan shrugged. She glanced around at the other girls to see if they understood what she was asking Aunt Maggie about. Alison squeezed her hand and Heather raised up her arms in a ballerina pose. They really had gone on the same adventure! They had all met Aunt Maggie when she was a teenager!

Aunt Maggie looked at each of the girl's faces. She didn't wait for an answer. It seemed to be one of those questions that everyone knows the answer to.

Megan noticed that if Aunt Maggie was surprised by what the girls knew it didn't show on her face. That's what a great actress she is, Megan thought for the millionth time.

"I'm not sorry that I broke my leg," Aunt Maggie answered. "You can't live in regret. You have to look for the blessing in the misfortune. Does that make sense?"

Megan nodded her head. "It's how you became a great actress."

Aunt Maggie said, "But this morning I just want to be a great aunt. So help me get down the bowls."

"Do you have raisins for the oatmeal?" Keisha asked.

"Absolutely not!" Aunt Maggie replied. "My oatmeal is the best with brown sugar and butter and a bit of maple syrup."

The sun was shining brightly through the kitchen windows as Megan and Aunt Maggie joined hands with the other girls to say a word of thanks. Aunt Maggie said she was grateful for the warm sun and crisp clean air of a brand-new day and all the opportunity it holds. Megan added that she was thankful for her four new best friends. Keisha said she wished there were raisins for the oatmeal, but she was happy there was creamy butter and maple syrup. Aunt Maggie opened her eyes and looked over at Keisha. Then she winked at her.

The girls helped Aunt Maggie dish up six warm, delicious bowls of oatmeal that tasted wonderful with the large cups of icy cold orange juice. Monty sat up on his hind legs for one of the dog biscuits that Aunt Maggie held out to him. Keisha looked out the window and said, "The streets have been plowed and are clear and Luis Delgado is outside shoveling the sidewalk."

"Yes," said Aunt Maggie. "Your families have all called this morning and are on their way to pick you up. Finish your breakfast. It's time to clean up the attic and get dressed."

As the girls were up in the attic folding up the blankets and putting the pillows away, Heather said, a little shyly, "I hope we can stay in touch. I have a hard time making new friends because my family moves so much."

Keisha said, "You can count on me being your friend. I'll give you my phone number and my email."

"Me, too," said Alison.

Megan had an idea. "Let's form a club, so we'll always know each other even though we don't live in the same neighborhoods."

"Good idea," Rosa said, "especially since we took such a great adventure together."

"What will we call the club?" asked Alison.

"What about the Magic Attic Club?" Aunt Maggie offered. Everyone was startled for a moment because they hadn't heard her come up the stairs.

"Really?" Megan asked. "Could we have our club meetings here?"

The girls all looked at Aunt Maggie with hope.

"I suppose you girls could have magic attic sleepovers here at my house," Aunt Maggie answered, with a sly smile.

"Yeah! Yeah!" the girls shouted, leaping up and down with excitement.

"But," Aunt Maggie said sternly, "only if there is no more getting lost, shaving or fainting involved."

All the girls laughed and ran over to Aunt Maggie, hugging her around the waist.

"Hurry now, girls," she freed herself from their embraces. "Your parents are waiting for you downstairs."

The girls all said goodbye to each other, exchanged phone numbers and email information, and went to meet their families. Keisha's dad was there to pick her up. With him was her two-year-old brother, Ronnie, who was playing on the floor, tossing a ball for Monty.

Rosa's Nana had come for her. She was not much taller than Rosa.

Alison pointed out the window at her twin brothers waiting in the car. As she pulled on her snow boots, she said, "See you all later. You're the best, Aunt Maggie."

Heather's mom was there, too, and held Heather tightly to her side as she thanked Aunt Maggie for letting her spend the night.

Megan was glad to see her own mom, and so was Aunt Maggie. Aunt Maggie called Megan's mom "baby" as they hugged and made plans to have lunch the next time she was in the city.

Megan pulled on her coat and was buttoning the top button when she remembered she was still wearing the key.

"Oh, here's the key, Aunt Maggie," Megan said. "Thanks for the greatest slumber party ever."

Aunt Maggie took the key and put it in a cherrywood box on the hallway table, right next to her favorite humanitarian award.

"We'll just leave it right there for the next time you come over," she said. "In the meantime, don't forget to use your imagination."

"I won't," Megan promised.

When Megan and her mom got down to the sidewalk a snowball flew through the air and hit Megan right in the back, but not very hard.

"Are you going to cry?" Megan heard someone say right next to her ear.

It was Kyle Dresden.

Megan scooped up a handful of snow and pushed it down the neck of his sweater.

"Hey!" shouted Kyle. "No fair!"

"Both of you get in the car," Megan's mother said, pretending to be mad. "And don't bring in any snow."

Once Megan and Kyle were both in the back seat with their seat belts on, Kyle told her about his fun night at Mr. Preston's.

"We had a blast!" Kyle bragged. "We played video games and made popcorn and giant chocolate chip cookies with Mrs. Preston. What did you girls do?"

"Oh, not much," Megan said. "We just went to Colorado Springs to where the Olympic ice skaters train."

"Yeah, right," Kyle said, rolling his eyes. "Sure."

From the front seat, Megan's mom said, "It sounds like your imagination is running wild, Megan. Be real, now. You know you couldn't have gone to Colorado Springs."

"Okay," Megan said. "You don't have to believe it."

Kyle zipped open his backpack and pulled out a large chocolate chip cookie wrapped in cellophane.

"Here," he said. "I made you one, since you gave me yours yesterday."

Megan looked at the cookie, which had a large letter "T" in blue frosting in the center.

"What's the letter 'T' for?" she asked.

Kyle started to laugh and said, "What do you think, Troll girl?"

Kyle laughed louder and louder until Megan's mom said, "Settle down, please."

Megan didn't really want to smile at Kyle's teasing, but she couldn't help it. Maybe her mom was right. Maybe Kyle really did like her. After all, he made her a cookie.

Megan opened the cellophane and broke off a piece for Kyle and one for her mom. Right before she took a bite, because she would never, ever let food and words come out of her mouth at the same time, she said, "Thanks, Kyle Crocodile."

The End

Discover More Magic!

You can enjoy every adventure of the Magic Attic just by reading all the books. And there's more!

You can have a whole world of Fun, Friends, and Imagination with the dolls, outfits, and accessories that are based on the books. And since Alison, Heather, Keisha, Megan, and Rosa can wear one another's clothes, you can relive their adventures, or create new ones of your own!

Visit us at www.MagicAtticClub.com to find out more about the exciting world of Magic Attic, or call our toll-free number for a retailer in your area: 1-800-775-9272.